CU00879734

Brutal Question

Brutal Question

Oliver Weld Bayer

"There is one question which we seldom ask each other directly: it is too brutal. And yet it is the only question worth asking. . . ."

Christopher Isherwood

COACHWHIP PUBLICATIONS
Greenville, Ohio

For Helen and Walter

Brutal Question, by Oliver Weld Bayer
© 2021 Coachwhip Publications edition

First published 1947
Oliver Weld Bayer was the pseudonym used by writing pair
    Eleanor Bayer (1914-1981) and Leo Grossfeld Bayer
    (n.d.-1950).
CoachwhipBooks.com

ISBN 1-61646-506-9
ISBN-13 978-1-61646-506-3

1

I ought to mark that day and remember it and celebrate every year when it rolls around, have a cake with candles, or go on a binge, or fast and meditate, though none of these is precisely appropriate. It's a day that belongs to me now—like another birthday. But that sounds too elaborate. There must be a word for the day when one's life turns a corner and heads down a strange new road that wasn't even on the map before. It must happen to a lot of people; it must be sung about in songs and whispered in confessions. It must be told about in stories.

I used to tell stories over the radio. Three nights a week for a quarter hour I sat in front of a microphone and spun yarns on a show called *Teller of Tales*. But that was before the war, and this business about life turning a corner happened after the war, when I was broadcasting six street interviews a week for the Logan Jewelry Company in Washington, D.C., and doing odd jobs for the network.

It started in August, shortly after V-J Day—the day I heard Harvey Benson was dead and saw Martha again, the day which began with the Bureau chap playing his little joke on me in the morning and ended with the dream I had in the night. These last two incidents are unconnected with what happened, but they belong to that day—they helped make it a big twenty-four hours.

First the morning. That summer in Washington I lived on Tilden Street near the Bureau of Standards, a place surrounded by guards and barbed wire where all sorts of secret military research was going on. Since it was too hot to sleep I got up early every day and walked down to a Connecticut Avenue drugstore for breakfast. Every morning exactly at the same time I passed a lean hatchet-faced character going to work at the Bureau. Under his arm he carried a shoe box tied with a string and containing, I supposed, his lunch. He ignored my nods for a week, and when a few more friendly attempts on my part brought no response I gave up. We continued to pass each other regularly in dour silence.

But that morning as we came abreast he looked straight into my eyes and uttered a short shrill laugh. Then he removed the shoe box from under the arm closest to me, put it with elaborate caution under his other arm, and walked on, grinning. Later when I was drinking my coffee I read in the *Post* that a famous scientist had just the day before assured a Senate committee that enough material to make an atom bomb could be carried in a shoe box.

It was a damn weird way to start a day.

In the afternoon I stood on top of our mobile unit parked at the corner of Constitution and Fifteenth and broadcast an eyewitness report of the big victory parade. I must have had a meager number of listeners in the Capital at least, for crowds packed the sidewalks downtown, and leaned from every available window and rooftop. Hundreds of small boys, needled with parade drug, poured like molasses past the restraining ropes along the curbs. Over us all hung limp flags, red, white, and blue buntings, and a broiling August sun.

"This is Alexander Pike," I said into the microphone. "For the past hour you have been receiving a play-by-play account of the great parade now taking place in Washington, D.C. That roar of applause you hear now is for three cars full of Congressional Medal of Honor men. They are waving and smiling. One of the young heroes just stood up and blew a kiss toward the crowd. I'm sure it was to the prettiest girl in town. He deserves her."

Even as I went on to describe the Marine Band coming next I wondered what had made me say that, what had brought out all the rest of the threadbare patriotic lingo I had been mouthing all afternoon. I was ashamed of myself for giving in to the parade, for letting the brassy blare of the bands and the tramp of marching feet get me. Those two late and great parade givers of Europe knew what they were doing, I guess. It takes a lot of the vaccine of cynicism to resist a show like that—more than I had, apparently.

The final section of the parade was captured Jap stuff, a suicide-plane and a battered landing craft, both with a surprisingly human air of humiliation. I described the last cars as they turned the corner toward the grandstand where the speeches were to be made.

"In a few minutes," I said into the microphone, "we are going to drive our mobile unit through the crowds here and let some of these people tell you how it feels to be a part of this happy and historic day. I return you now to studio headquarters."

When I climbed down into the truck I heard Hal talking to Wellman through the transmitter.

"I felt like a fried egg up there," I told him. "Did Wellman hear me sizzle?"

Hal took off his headphones and got into the driver's seat beside me. "He said it was okay. Good coverage. Now where?"

"Now find me some people."

"What's wrong with right here?"

"Plenty," I said bitterly. I reached up my back and
detached my seersucker jacket from the damp patch on my
shirt, and my shirt from where it was plastered against my
spine. "For Christ sake, the next time you park this thing,
find some shade."

Hal made a left turn and started slowly up Fifteenth.
"Ain't no cooler in the shade," he announced with the
complacence of long experience. "Shade or sun, it's all the
same. Seems to be gettin' worse though. Didn't *used* to be
so hot."

I knew what he was leading up to. Harold Corbett was
a plump little man about fifty years old, and to look at
him you wouldn't think he was any different from anyone
else. But he had taken care to assure me that he was indeed a rare creature. In a town where the standard greeting is "Where you from?" he was a native. Born and bred
in D.C. He was a radio engineer by profession, but his
real career was nostalgia. All summer since I'd been doing
street interviews with the mobile unit he'd filled my ears
with laments for the Washington that used to be, for that
quiet untrammeled country village which, to hear him tell
it, had been populated entirely by gracious waitresses and
polite bus drivers.

"It never *seemed* so hot," he was saying now, his round
face studded with sweat and prickly heat. He nosed the
truck around a gang of sailors and their girls who'd locked
arms and gone into the parade business for themselves.
"Wasn't so many durn furriners runnin' around bumpin'
into each other, packin' into places—"

"Don't stop," I said. "Explain to me how the New Deal
changed the climate here too."

"Reckon if you'd been here in the old days you'd know
I'm right."

"My life's been lived too late," I said. "I didn't see London till it was blitzed by the Germans. I didn't see Paris

till it was occupied by the Germans. Now you tell me I didn't see Washington till it was both—by the Democrats."

We turned down Pennsylvania Avenue into a traffic jam involving some streetcars which looked as if they weren't going to be moving for a while. Hal shut off the motor and we waited.

"I wish I could check up on you," I said. "I wish I'd come down here about fifteen years ago, when I had the chance."

"Why didn't you?"

"The trip was a prize for the best American history paper in the eighth grade. Friend of mine, boy by the name of Harvey Benson, won."

"Harvey Benson. There used to be a news analyst down here by that name."

"That's the one."

"Did you go to school with him?"

"Sure, he's from Cleveland. Next time I run into him I'll find out what kind of a liar you are, Hal."

"Not from him you won't. He's dead."

"That's too bad," I said. "I hadn't heard. Moving around so much, I lost track—" I'd heard about a great many other people dying in the past few years and I'd seen a share of them at it, but Benson I hadn't heard about.

I started to ask how it had happened, when with a loud whoop a girl leaped from the streetcar loading platform onto our running board. Her long hair was parted and combed like some movie star's.

"Mistuh Radio Man," she screamed in a deep-South accent, "kin Ah say hello to muh boy friend ovah the radio? Kin Ah send muh boy friend a lovin' message ovah theah to Guam?"

"Try a letter, honey," said Hal. "The air's censored. Step down now, honey."

She made a pout out of her lipsticked mouth and got back on the platform. Standing there in her white blouse and flowered dirndl skirt, she didn't look like any movie actress at all. She looked like the kind of kid the town was full of—lonely, and far from home.

"More trash in Washington these days," muttered Hal. He inched the truck along the car tracks.

"What happened," I asked, "to Benson?"

"Can't rightly recall now. Read it in the paper—I reckon it was a year ago. It seems he was over in Italy with some USO act—I didn't know he was an actor too."

"He wasn't an actor. He couldn't get into the service for physical reasons and he didn't want to be a correspondent. He told me he wanted to do something more—more direct for the men overseas, so he took an assignment as master of ceremonies with a USO act. What happened in Italy?"

"He drowned himself in one of those Italian lakes. Committed suicide. Lake Fucino, I think it said."

"That's impossible! I don't believe it!" I exploded. "At least," I added in a milder tone, "I knew him pretty well. I can't imagine him committing suicide. He just—he just wasn't the type."

"I said the same thing to myself when I read it. Now what would a smart up-and-comin' guy want to go and do that for? Young, too, wasn't he?"

"My age."

Hal swore at the streetcars and turned his attention to getting past them. He drew up beside a triangle of grass in front of the National Theater and parked in the thin band of shade along its curb. I sat there feeling depressed and curiously angry about Harvey Benson. It was a weak protest to say he wasn't the type to kill himself. Possibly we all are the type if life gets unbearable enough. But what had happened to him? A vision of his slender undersized body floating on the sapphire-blue water of "one of those Italian lakes" crossed my mind. His eyes were closed in his narrow face and he was almost bald, the way he'd been the last time I saw him. But the queer thing in my vision was that he lay there in the water wearing a gray sweat shirt and track shorts. I hadn't time to wonder why. Hal was calling in to tell Wellman where we were and that we'd be ready at three-thirty. I heard him asking what the Senators had done to the Red Sox at the end of the inning.

I got out of the truck, wishing my stint were done with and I could get to a shower. As usual, as soon as we parked a crowd clustered around to watch. It was my job to pick out three of the spectators to take part in the broadcast. Early in the summer when I was still green at doing the interviews I had an unsteady feeling looking at all the faces. My insides would start snarling up and the nerve in my cheek begin to quiver, and I'd wonder what the hell I'd do if no one agreed to come up and be interviewed. But there wasn't any need for this anxiety. Wherever I stood with my microphone there were always too many people willing and eager to talk about themselves or their opinions over the air. In the couple of months I'd been doing it I had developed an instinct about people. I was good at selecting the ones who would give the most on the broadcast. All this is to explain that if I'd been paying attention that day of the parade I'd never have lighted on the chap in the tan polo shirt—never.

But after I saw Martha—and I saw her the instant I started to focus on individuals in the crowd around me—I wasn't paying attention to much else. I recognized her right away, though the smart black dress and hat she had on were a far cry from that phony uniform she'd worn in France. But her face was the same. Suddenly I realized I'd been looking into every crowd everywhere for that face, carrying with me a memory of it sharp as a photograph. It struck me as completely crazy that I should find it there on a wastepaper-cluttered street corner in Washington, D.C. One night about a year before I'd spent several minutes considering appropriate places where one might find that face.

"Maybe we'll meet again back in the States," she had said.

I recognized the foolishness of making plans there in the dark with the noise of the big guns somewhere past Nancy sounding closer than they were, but I wanted to do it anyway. The woman with me was fresh from another world: her hair had been washed in New York less than a week before; she came from a back-home place which must still exist and she would return to it. So must I, I thought for the first time. If she'd say something to show she believed I would return it might be a kind of promise that I would. Superstitiously all I needed was to hear her say it.

"Yes, let's meet," I agreed. "Where in the States is one apt to meet you, Mrs. Finchley?"

I had an idea where. In those smart hotel elevators smelling of perfume and good leather luggage, in the crush of key holders waiting to be lifted to their glass-walled showers and room-service push buttons, there, sleek and expectant, would be Mrs. Finchley. *Why, good morning— it's Mrs. Finchley!* Or in the fashionable restaurant, her dark fur with its impeccable label slung over her chair, the impeccable wine in its silver bucket on the table. *Good evening, Mrs. Finchley!* In the penthouse of the powerful publisher who'd sent her overseas, in the shop of the famous designer who'd created that dining-at-officers-club dress in her duffel. *Hello, if it isn't Mrs. Finchley!* What would I be doing in any of those places where perhaps we'd meet again?

I asked her that question.

"You're here, aren't you?" she said, "And I'm here. If we met at home, say at cocktails, and discussed the possibility

of running into each other in France you'd have thought
it just as unlikely."

"But you wouldn't have?"

I felt the shrug of her smooth shoulder under my hand.
"Even left to itself life is unexpected. I believe in giving
it a little help."

"All right," I said, "you can always reach me through
my agent, Stanley Day, in New York City, or my father,
R. T. Pike, in Cleveland."

"That's a help."

"There's an Alexander Pike listed in Cleveland, too,
but it's not me. It's my ex-wife."

"Oh? So you were always hard to get along with?"

"It was fifty-fifty. But by the time we caught on we had
a kid. Stevie's living with my parents now. I'll show you
his photograph when we get back to camp."

"I'd like to see it." Her voice sounded as if she meant
it, but that was all she said—she didn't offer any information about herself. I realized I didn't even know where
she lived back home, and though I wanted to question her
some sort of queer pride kept me silent.

She leaned over and picked her jacket up from the
floor, searching in its pocket for cigarettes. I remembered
the circular green insignia on its sleeve: war correspondent. Mrs. Finchley-who-mustn't-miss-anything, playing
make-believe reporter of the wars. What was it she had told
the colonel? "I want to write about the small human-inter-
est details that aren't in the big dispatches. I want to make
the people reading about a war at home feel exactly as if
they were here. I want to see and do everything."

I don't know what the boss thought about this speech.
(It was repeated to me by a corporal on the switchboard
at HQ who had a picturesque term for what he thought
of it.) At any rate, for the past twenty-four hours I and a

jeep had been assigned to aid Mrs. Finchley in her worthy research. We didn't miss much either.

"How do you intend to write this up in your column?" I asked her. "Take heart, girls! War hasn't made a nasty psychoneurotic out of your boy friend. I spent last night with a plain GI Joe. Underneath the whiskers and the grime your soldier is still filled with tender regard for American Womanhood—"

She propped herself up on her elbow and struck a match.

I had used these same matches earlier. They were from the Waldorf-Astoria. The flame lighted her face and threw the shadow of her profile on the splintery boards that covered the window. She was smiling.

"Is that how you imagine yourself?" she asked. "Listen, my dear boy, you don't have to be so bright and brittle. I really didn't come here with you to get material for my column."

"I know what you came for."

I got up and walked across the room and lighted the kerosene lamp. It was standing on a drawerless chest which was the only whole piece of furniture in the place. When the house had been used as a billet someone had pinned a photograph above the chest, a picture of a long-haired blonde in a black evening dress. Slightly askew on a single thumbtack, she stared archly at me now. I went back and held my cigarette to Martha's until it caught. Then I sat down and looked at her. Her face was—was different from that pin-up blonde's, for example. It had an off-beat kind of beauty that demanded attention. Slightly protuberant brown eyes, straight nose, strong mouth and chin—it was a face that had stood up to about forty years of life already, and it didn't seem to be asking any questions. Her thick red-brown hair hung loose now almost to her shoulders. I had seen it in the daylight streaked with gray, coiled smoothly on her neck, beneath her overseas cap.

Contemplating her, my contempt and resentment vanished. Who was I to criticize the life she led? Whatever the reason, she was here in the cold and dirt and with me. Tomorrow she'd be gone and I'd never see her again—that was what mattered.

"Martha," I said, "to hell with back in the States. I'm due for a forty-eight-hour pass next week end. Will you meet me in Nancy?"

"How can I? I'm supposed to be in Rome next week end."

"You don't have to be. Those PROs have so many correspondents to nurse they won't miss you. They'll think you got hung up somewhere."

"It's not a PRO who's expecting me." For a moment she stared across the room and her eyes glowed yellow with the reflection of the dim kerosene flame. "My dear boy," she said, "it's absolutely impossible, but I think I'm going to try."

We made a date to meet at a café, a big gay place in the center of the city that everyone knew about and visited.

"And cut out the dear boy," I said. "Have I been so boyish tonight? Have I not measured up to your standard of maturity?"

"Oh yes, darling," she said. "You have."

Of course she didn't show up in Nancy. I ran into some friends of mine in the café who were with a Red Cross girl who'd gone to Smith with my cousin, and we all had a sort of American collegiate two days together.

The next time I saw Martha was on that Washington street corner in front of the National Theater.

2

She was staring at me with a queer mixture of impersonal-ity and interest, the way she might regard a performing bear. As for me, I felt as I had during the parade when the drums turned my insides into an answering, pulsing drumbeat and I felt the same shame at being so vulnerable. Abruptly I looked away from her, and then I saw this blond fellow with the sunburned face and lively blue eyes and the sunburned chest showing at the V of his tan polo shirt.

"We'd like our listeners to hear what some of you people think of the victory celebration," I said to him. "Would you answer a few questions over the air, sir?"

He stepped forward. "Why, sure. Go ahead and ask, brother." I should have known by the way he held himself, his arms crooked belligerently out from his sides, that he'd be troublesome.

"Thanks," I said. "If you'll wait just a minute, please, we're not quite ready to go on." Hurriedly I picked a marine private with a starred ETO ribbon and a young woman, on her way to catch a bus to Kecoughtan, who said she'd be thrilled to talk over the radio because her husband at Walter Reed might be listening. By that time Hal had held up his hand and we were on the air.

I spoke into the microphone, giving our position and describing the scene in the street, the ankle-deep paper scraps, the Good Humor stand doing a rush business, and, opposite us, the firemen dismantling an arch that had been made for the parade out of two hundred-foot ladders.

"We've cornered some of the celebrants," I announced, "and we're going to ask them to tell you how it feels to be down here on this great historic day." I turned to the blond fellow beside me.

"Would you tell us your name and address, please?"

"George Harbin. I live here." He eyed the mike in my hand as if it might dispute him.

"And what is your occupation, Mr. Harbin?"

"That's my own private business, brother." His light blue gaze flickered over the crowd with the same expectancy of challenge.

"You watched the parade, Mr. Harbin. What do you think of the way Washington is celebrating the home-coming of its heroes?"

"I was mighty glad to see all those machine guns and rifles. I feel more comfortable knowin' we got 'em in this country ready for when we need 'em. If you ask me, brother, were going to be needin' 'em—"

"Could you see the general from where you were standing, Mr. Harbin?" I interrupted. "What sort of man did he look like to you?"

"Puh-lenty tough, brother. Full of the old know-how. He's the kind of guy we're goin' to need. We licked the Germans and Japs, but now we got to lick another crumby bunch right in this country. Certain un-American elements, and you know who I mean, are goin' to be swingin' from—"

I took his arm. "Thank you very much, Mr. Harbin. Now if you'll step aside, please." I held the mike out to the marine. "Your name, Private?"

"Lookit here, brother," protested Harbin, snatching his arm away from me and butting his elbow into my side at the same time. "I'm not through talkin'. I jist want to say that—"

"We can talk later," I told him. "We're on the air now."

"My name's Private Milton Collingwood, United States Marine Corps," said the marine. "I'm from—"

"That's what I want to do—talk over the air!" shouted Mr. Harbin. "I'm not afraid to say what I think! I know my rights! Say, what's your name, anyway?"

I glanced over my shoulder at Hal. He scowled at me and spoke into the transmitter. Again I took hold of Harbin with my free hand and tried to lead him aside.

"I'm from Mount Carroll, Illinois," said the marine into the dead mike. "I'd like to say hello to all the folks in Mount Carroll—"

Harbin twisted from my grasp, his eyes squinting up into mine. "You think you're pretty big, don'tcha, brother? How'd you like to get cut down to your right size?"

Someone shouted a warning. As he drew back his arm I ducked and his fist grazed the side of my head. The marine left off greeting Mt. Carroll and rushed at him, pinioning his arms from behind. He hustled his prisoner through the crowd across the sidewalk and onto the grass. I caught a glimpse of the tussle, before too many people closed in around them. I signaled to Hal.

"The display of military might this afternoon seems to have put our first guest into a fighting mood," I said into the mike. "Now we have here a young woman from Kecoughtan who has been in Washington visiting her husband at Walter Reed Hospital. Will you tell us your name, please?"

But the woman had her hand to her mouth. "Oh, I couldn't say a word," she gasped. "Oh, that awful person. Oh, I'm just too nervous to talk; you'll have to excuse me."

"Would I do for an interview?" The voice challenged me. It was, as I remembered it, a voice like that of an actress with a talent for choosing the right note for every emotion. "I'll be glad to answer any questions." Her face was turned up to me, sly and amused.

I felt the perspiration streaking down my own. Why, yes, I thought, when strangers meet there are always questions. Who are you and how did you get here and what have you been doing with your life until now? But we are a little less than strangers. Do you remember the farmhouse with the crazy jackstraws of trees in its front yard? Do you remember the faded improbable roses blooming on the wallpaper inside? "For the rest of my life when I see roses . . ." you said. Have you been in a garden lately, Mrs. Finchley? Why, yes, I thought, there are some things I'd like to ask. . . .

"Your name, please?" I asked.

"Mrs. Oscar M. Finchley."

"Is Washington your home, Mrs. Finchley?"

"Not originally, but my husband was in business here. When he died just before the war, I stayed on and now I feel like a native."

"Then you like the Capital?"

"It's a fascinating place to live. There's no city to equal it in the world. Oh, maybe Paris, but—"

"Have you been to Paris recently?"

"I was there last year—on a reporting assignment."

"Then you're a writer?"

"Not exactly. I've always been interested in journalism."

"Did you get to any of the other French cities? Nancy, for example?"

"No. Never to Nancy, much to my regret."

"That's a shame, Mrs. Finchley. A real shame." I glanced toward Hal. He held up three fingers. Three more minutes. "Suppose you tell us what you thought of the big parade today."

"Undoubtedly the fanciest parade this city has ever held."

"Now," I said, "just because we haven't had enough excitement this afternoon, let me ask you to go out on a limb in front of all the boys in uniform standing around here and tell us which branch of the service you think put on the best show."

"Not having seen any of them, I couldn't tell you."

"But I thought—"

"To be perfectly honest, Mr. Pike, I couldn't get near enough to see anything. I parked my car over there"—she gestured toward the lot behind the District Building—"and listened to your broadcast."

I laughed. It was said to be a good radio laugh. At any rate, my sponsor, Mr. Ralph Logan, president of the Logan Jewelry Company, liked it. He had a theory that people bought more diamonds when they were happy. "Laugh," he was always telling me, "project a light mood." "Asking you about the parade, Mrs. Finchley, is going to be like asking myself."

"Try me and see. I think my reactions were quite different." She smiled at the crowd.

"Suppose you tell us your reactions."

"I ought to explain," she said, "that they are influenced by the fact that as a child I saw this same kind of parade when the last war ended—a date when you, Mr. Pike, were probably a babe in arms."

"You're wrong. I stood up in my carriage and waved a flag. I was very precocious."

"At any rate, my enthusiasm is neither as fresh nor as unlimited as yours. Two world wars and two victory parades—I think we're getting in a rut."

"But it's a winning rut. Do you object to that?"

"I object to all ruts. They're boring and dangerous. Now that this war is over, we might avoid another one by doing things differently from last time. No parades for the victors, for example, no short-memory sympathy for the losers, no useless marble monuments for the dead. I want to start an Anti-Monument Committee. Any joiners?"

"I'm very sorry," I said. "Our time is up. Thank you for talking to us, Mrs. Finchley, and best of luck to you with your committee. I think it's a fine idea."

The crowd whistled and applauded. I saw the marine who had disposed of my assailant edging toward the microphone and clapping his hands for her. His shirt was dusty and his left eye puffed and bruised.

After I'd made the routine closing announcement and we were off the air I turned to him.

"How's that eye?" I asked. "I certainly feel responsible for it."

He touched the discolored flesh with his finger. "It's nothing, sir."

"Where's the blond bombshell?"

He jerked his thumb toward the other side of the street. "He doesn't feel like talking so much any more."

"It was damn good of you to help me out. Look, how about coming over to the Willard and having a drink with me?"

"No thanks, sir. I've got to hurry down to the station and catch a train. I got a girl waiting for me at home. At least she said she'd wait." He frowned. "War changes things a lot, though. That's why I couldn't appreciate hearing that jackass talk up another one." He grinned and saluted and disappeared down the thronged sidewalk.

Martha and I were left facing each other.

"Hello, Alec," she said.

"Hello."

"Didn't I foretell this? Didn't I say we'd meet again in the States?"

"You're uncanny. You ought to pitch a tent and give readings."

The horn blew long and insistent from the truck.

"That's for me," I said.

"Must you go back to the station now? Can I drive you? I'd like to repay some chauffeuring you did for me once."

"Wait a minute," I said. We were through with this broadcast and I had nothing scheduled until my own program the following day. I went over to the truck and told Hal to go on without me. He rolled his eyes at Martha.

"What you goin' to do?" he whispered. "Become a charter member?"

I didn't see why I should explain anything to him. I put the mike on the seat beside him and slammed the door.

"So long, fat boy," I said.

"So long, ole bean, ole kid."

3

Her car turned out to be a Pontiac station wagon with a Maryland license and the initials L.M.S. on the door. The back seats were piled with bundles of clothing tied with twine.

"These are for Belgian Relief," she said. "I borrowed this wagon to pick them up. That's how I happened to hear you today. I don't have a radio in my own car."

We drove out onto Pennsylvania Avenue, still jammed with the traffic aftermath of the parade. "I have one more bundle to pick up in Georgetown, and then suppose we go through the park and try to find a breeze."

"Okay," I said, stretching out my legs and relaxing. "I want to see and do everything."

She smiled. "I can't promise you as exciting a tour as you produced for me last year."

I wondered what she felt about last year. Beside me in her thin black dress, her face as cool and as delicately colored as a ceramic mask, her hair drawn back over the lustrous pearl in her ear lobe, she seemed another woman altogether. This was her back-home-in-America look that I had once conjured up to offend myself.

"Anyway," she was saying, "you've probably seen more of Washington this summer than I have in all the years I've been here. I've listened to you interview people in places all over town that I didn't know existed. I'm a fan of yours, by the way."

"Are you?" I asked. "Are you a woman of exquisite discrimination?" I mimicked the tone of my commercial. "Do you select your gems at one of Logan's five convenient stores eager to serve you in five convenient locations? Are you in the forefront of fashion? Do you own tomorrow's earring today?"

She laughed. "I bet Ralph Logan writes those little pieces himself. I used to know him. He's a fool." She glanced at me. "I hope he isn't paying you too much."

"What he pays me plus what I get for special broadcasts like today's amount to—the salary of a second lieutenant. Why? Do I lose my charm as I acquire rank?"

"I'm going to make you a proposition and I wouldn't want you to be able to afford to turn it down."

At this intriguing point in our conversation we drove up to a three-story red brick house on one of the streets off Wisconsin Avenue in Georgetown. A colored man in a white coat opened the door.

"Hello, Clayton," Martha called. "I've come for Mrs. Langley's bundle for Belgian relief."

"Yes, ma'am." He went back inside.

"Who is Mrs. Langley?" I asked.

"Her husband's Chester Langley, the one who's something big in reconversion. Was, rather. He resigned yesterday."

"Darling!" A slender dark woman in flame-colored pajamas came around the house toward us, arms outstretched. "Aren't you cute in that little station wagon. Whose is it? Lloyd's?"

"Yes," said Martha. "This is Mr. Pike. Mrs. Langley."

Mrs. Langley put one foot on the running board and tossed a dazzling smile in on me. "Isn't she the hardest little worker, Mr. Pike?" She peered into my eyes with her own well-glazed black ones. "I declare, she makes me ashamed of myself. Martha Finchley, I don't have my bundle ready! Aren't I awful?" The scent of rum and perfume wafted over us.

"Tomorrow's the deadline for the shipment," Martha told her. "Maybe you can send Clayton over with it in the morning."

"Oh, but, darling, I won't have time to go through my things by then! Isn't it ghastly? The Rossinis are coming for cocktails any minute now." She patted my arm. "Come on around and join us on the terrace."

Martha shook her head. "No, thanks, Estelle, we really can't."

"And then there's the Cottermans' dinner afterward and that Fernandez reception at the Sulgrave after that. And the phone ringing all the time—reporters wanting to know why Chet resigned. They're such tiresome bastards," she said thoughtfully. Her eyes swung slowly into focus on me. "Are you a reporter, darling?"

"No," I said.

"They simply won't accept facts. Chet *tells* them and *tells* them it's not political. Just that we want to live our own quiet little life. Now you two sweets must come with me. Claytons making frosted daiquiris—"

Martha turned on the ignition. "We've got to run along, Estelle, honestly—"

Mrs. Langley let her hands drop to her sides. It was clear that we were tiresome too. Then the initials on the car door reminded her of something.

"Let's all drive out to Lloyd's together on Labor Day," she said. "You and Carlos come here for a cocktail first. Darling, did you notice that the cards said dancing! When Clayton came back to us I thought the war was over, but a dancing party at the Seabrights' again! Now I'm sure the war is over! Good-by, you two sweets." She waved merrily as we drove off.

When we had turned the corner I said, "Affectionate, isn't she?"

Martha gave me a sidelong glance. "Don't count on it," she said. "She talked to me like that the first time we met, but I had to be introduced to her in nine different places before she remembered me." Her tone was mildly bitter. "It was a tough fight, Mother." She turned her attention back to the driving, and I watched her white fingers as they guided the wheel. The nails were flawlessly lacquered; the skin looked smooth to touch. I was thinking we had met again, on a street corner far from France, and we had not even shaken hands.

"Light me a cigarette, will you?"

I took a fresh pack of Chesterfields out of my pocket and pulled at the thin red band of cellophane. I wanted to ask her why she had cared about her status with Mrs. Langley and who was Lloyd, the gentleman of the station wagon and dancing parties, and who was Carlos. When she reached for her cigarette I noticed an oddly carved heavy silver bracelet on her wrist—not the sort of merchandise offered in Logan's five convenient stores.

"That's an exotic trinket," I said.

"Isn't it? A friend of mine picked it up in Buenos Aires."

Who? I wanted to ask her. What friend?

We drove down into the leafy-smelling warmth of Rock Creek Park. No breeze could have gotten through that thicket of foliage, but the shade gave us an illusion of relief. Martha pulled off the road into a parking space beside a deserted grill and picnic table. No one was around. Nearby the children's swings hung motionless in the sun.

We got out of the car and walked to the bank of the creek where the water flowed slow and smooth and almost

black. Martha took off her hat and sat down on a large
rock.

"This is one of the loveliest spots in the park," she said.

"Where are we?"

"Just below the Equitation Field. I often ride down
here."

"I've missed this trail. I've been exploring them all on
Sunday mornings."

"Do you like to ride?" she asked. "Do you keep a horse
down here?"

"On a second lieutenant's salary?" I shook my head.
"I hire mine by the hour from Charlie Thurston. He's a
colored fellow who has a stable on Oak Road just off Sixteenth Street."

"I don't know that one. I keep mine over at the Fieldstone Club. My husband gave me a wonderful Irish hunter—"

"Maybe we can get together for a ride sometime. I'd—"

"Maybe." She cut me off and changed the subject
abruptly. "You look fine in civvies."

"So do you."

"Tell me what's happened to you since—since the last
time I saw you."

"The usual things. I was wounded. I spent a long time
in the hospital. I was discharged. I found someone else
had my old job. I got this one."

"Were you badly hurt, Alec?" For the first time the
keep-your-distance amusement left her eyes.

"It wasn't much." I pointed to the long white scar.
"Caught a slug in my jaw. For a chap who makes his living
by talking, I was in a bad spot. Had to quit talking and
start thinking for a change."

"How did it happen?"

"Shortly after you turned down a chance to see the
historic city of Nancy, we were driving through Lunéville

when a joyful native shot off a gun in our honor. He was too blind-happy to care where he was aiming. It made an appropriate low-comedy ending to my military career."

"How did you happen to turn up here and go to work for Ralph Logan?"

"Logan's son heard me do some GI interviews in London and sold the old man the idea. I'd really enjoy doing the program if Papa wouldn't insist I do the commercials too. In his half-carat brain he thinks it's good for business to have me personally vouch for his diamonds. The best reason, however, is it's the only job I can find at the moment."

"Why didn't you go back to the *Teller of Tales* program?"

As if she'd struck a cymbal, her question set off vibrations of the old dull pain in my gut—the one that started when I got back to New York and for the first time listened to Jack Wininger do the show. He'd taken over my inflections, my mannerisms, my method of handling the material, and, to top it, his Hooper rating was double mine.

The next morning Stan had lost some of his radio agent's slick assurance when he explained things to me.

"About Jack's new contract," he said. "I wouldn't have let it go through if I'd known the war would be over." The way he said that, the way too many people at home were saying that, infuriated me. I pointed to the newspaper on his desk. The headlines said: *Japanese Suicide Plane Damages U. S. Carrier.*

"I mean the war in Europe," he said quickly. "I mean that you'd be getting back; I mean getting discharged—"

I helped him out. "You couldn't have known anything about it, Stan."

"What I think," he said, "is that you and I and Jack and the agency people ought to sit down and talk it over. We can explain the Hooper thing somehow—"

"What do you mean, somehow? I did all the pioneering. You know how long it takes before people realize there is a new show on the air and what it's all about. It stands to, reason the rating would go up by the time Jack took it—"

"Uh, that's right," he said. "And besides, we can tell them you're a veteran; you were over there fighting for this country. We can just appeal to their better nature, Alex. But you know how it is—a contract is a contract."

"Don't pull that stuff," I said. "I know you got a better deal for Jack than you could get for me now. I've been off the air for two years—I might as well be dead. Look, to Hell with it. I don't want to go back on that show. I want to do something else."

The sagging lines in Stan's puffy face turned upward. He took a bottle and a couple of glasses out of a cabinet. "You know," he said, "there'll be a lot of summer replacement shows kicking around pretty soon, maybe we can—"

"I want to do something altogether different," I said. "I don't want to sit alone in front of a mike any more. I want to do something with people, audience participation—"

"Quiz stuff?"

"No. Not who was vice-president in 1895, madame. Not like that. Maybe some sort of interview—really find out what keeps people going. I know what I mean, but I don't know how to—"

Stan looked at his watch. I had been in the office about ten minutes, and this was the third time he'd looked at it.

"Okay," he said. "Let's have lunch tomorrow and dream up some angles."

"What's wrong with now?"

"Jesus," he said, "I'm tied up. I'm supposed to be over at Columbia right now. I don't want to rush you, Alec, but—"

"But that's what you're doing." The thick rug made my walk to the door dreamy and painless. "I can't make it for

lunch tomorrow," I said. "I'm going down to Washington—and I don't know when I'll be back."

"Jesus, you aren't sore, are you?" I heard him call as the
door shut silently behind me like a door in a dream too.

"I never heard *Teller of Tales.*" Martha's voice broke
through to me. "When I mentioned your name the other
night several people told me you were wonderful. Why
didn't you go back?"

She was running her finger along the ridges of the rock,
and the links of her silver bracelet clicked softly with the
movement. My anger with the memory of that session in
Stan's office suddenly transferred itself to her. Why was I
allowing her to cross-examine me? She was an unknown
woman in an unknown world of her own, with her friends
who bought her gifts from Buenos Aires. What had she to
do with me really? If this was to be business, as she had
hinted, then let us dispense with my personal history and
get down to business.

"Suppose I take a turn at asking questions," I said.
"You mentioned a proposition?"

"All right. Let's talk about that. If I hadn't run into
you this afternoon I was going to telephone you tonight or
tomorrow. I want to offer you a job. A radio job on a new
show I'm ready to produce. I think it's a fresh, diverting
idea, but I need a good master of ceremonies to help put
it over. Someone who'll do as much for it as Fadiman, for
example, does for *Information Please.*"

"A quiz show?"

"No, there's nothing like it on the air. It's a really original idea—I'm sold on it. But it's got to have the right
m.c. or it won't go over."

"What makes you think I'm the guy?"

"I've been listening to you all summer. I like the way
you handle people, the things you say, your spontaneity.

Of course we can't tell how you'd work out until we try. Would you be interested?"

So now it is radio, I thought; last year it was reporting the war. Mrs. Finchley-who-mustn't-miss-anything. Why was it that she put this queer, resentful, defensive feeling in me now as she had the first time I was with her? A feeling that was a pressure in my throat and a hot jealous flicker behind my eyes. What the hell was wrong with me?

"I can make it very worthwhile if you turn out to be the person I'm looking for," she was saying. "I've lined up a half-hour on Sunday evening over a national network and a sponsor who's willing to pay whatever the show costs. This isn't going to be small-time stuff, Alec."

Of course not. When Martha Finchley wanted to take a look at war the biggest newspaper publisher in the East gave her a column of newsprint in which to tell about it. When Martha Finchley got an idea for a radio show she also and automatically got someone to foot the bill. A Sunday-evening spot on a national hookup. Some bill.

She was looking at me, her eyes intense under her straight dark brows. It means something to her, I thought; she's dead serious. Maybe she's really got an idea. Maybe it's an honest-to-God good show. This is a break she's offering me. And then I thought about my daily drool over the gaudy junk in Ralph Logan's five convenient stores. How long could I keep it up? How long could I implore his customers, the civil servants, the CAFs—1 to 10—the young men clerks, the young girl typists from the towns of Idaho or Georgia or Maine, to seal their love, their faltering, hopeful, rooming-house, housing-project love, with a diamond from Logan's? (Twelve-fifty down and the rest in easy payments.)

So what if it was a radio show this year? Why was I acting as if she had insulted me? This might turn out to be the chance I needed so much. What did I want of Martha? That she stay at home counting laundry? That she lunch for three hours at Pierre's or La Salle du Bois with some other idle women? Would I feel better if she were offering me a cheap little adventure instead? Far, far inside my head, behind a dozen locked doors in my brain, a quiet voice said, You're in love with her.

Still staring at me, Martha said, "We're supposed to go on next Sunday and we're desperate for help. We've done some trial runs. I have the recordings at home. I'd like you to hear them and get to work right away, if you're interested."

"I'm damn interested."

"Good. I'm tied up tonight, but will you come over tomorrow night about eight-thirty? I'll have my friends, the ones who are going to be in on this with me, there. We'll want your suggestions."

I offered her another cigarette and lit one for myself too.

"Give me some sort of idea about it, can't you?" I asked. "I know it's hard to put it over telling about it, but I'm curious, naturally."

"At the moment," she said, "the show's called *Sunday Night on S Street.* I live on S Street. For years, while my husband was alive and ever since, I've held a sort of buffet supper—open house every Sunday. Our friends brought their friends—you know how those things snowball. Our Sunday nights began to be talked about here, in New York, around the East, wherever our guests traveled. We achieved fame in the society columns and what not." She smiled. "I'm not aware of what sort of conversation goes on at Evalyn Walsh McLean's affairs. I've never been invited. But the conversation at my house is fabulous, marvelous. There's bound to be good talk at a good Washington party, don't you think?"

"Yes. Yes, of course," What was she going to tell me—that she wanted to make a radio program out of her own little social affairs? That she actually had the nerve to think a party at her home on S Street was something millions of people would even so much as turn a dial to get in on? That she intended to broadcast conversation?

She read my thoughts. "The people who come to my house are distinguished and prominent, nationally important, some of them. Everyone likes to listen to the talk and opinions of smart, interesting people, whose names are news. The show is based on the talk at my Sunday-night parties, spontaneous discussion—some serious, some quite frivolous—manipulated by me as hostess. But we've decided something's missing. I can't carry it myself. We need a good master of ceremonies and we need him quick. I have a library off the drawing room we plan to use for the broadcast—bring in a few people at a time, as if they'd stepped in to drink their coffee, or to find a book, or were just passing the door. We plan to have new guests every week and a panel of regulars to carry on the continuity: myself as hostess, Lloyd Seabright, and Enid Hoyt. Do you get what we're trying for, Alec?"

Suddenly the scene clicked for me. I had a swift, intriguing impression of its appeal: the gay, clamorous clatter of party in the background, the interviews, the give-and-take talk before the mike, the different types and sorts of people one could get, the projection of the spell and fascination of the city of Washington. She was right, everything depended on the interlocutor, the master of ceremonies. And it was different from anything else on the air. If it could be done right, with skill, if it could achieve just the proper tone—it would be a knockout.

"I think it's a swell idea," I told her, "and a damn original one. You're right about the m.c. He's got to be awfully, awfully good."

She stood up. "I've thought for a long time that you're our man, Alec, but Lloyd Seabright kept insisting we needed a big name. I told him Fadiman wasn't a name until *Information Please* got going."

"Lloyd who?"

"Lloyd Seabright. You've heard of him, haven't you? He was a special assistant in the State Department during the war."

"Oh yes. Yes, I think so," I said. Lloyd Seabright. I knew the name. I had seen it many times in many connections: wealthy Western family, sportsman, playboy, chairman of such-and-such a drive, director of such-and-such a foundation. Yes, even something about the State Department. My mind leaped through shadowy recollections of pictures: Lloyd Seabright and family in Palm Beach; Lloyd Seabright snapped at the Washington airport about to take off for —; reading from left to right, Lloyd M. Seabright, chairman; snapped among the guests at the wedding of the Ambassador; Mr. and Mrs. Lloyd Seabright . . .

"Lloyd's agreed to be one of my regulars," Martha was saying as we walked toward the car. "You'll meet him tomorrow night."

When we were still several yards from the parking space we saw that the small picnic ground had become crowded while we were sitting down near the creek. A half-dozen cars were drawn up beside the station wagon; baskets of food stood on the tables and a fire was burning in the grill. About twenty people were playing baseball on the grass nearby. We heard the whack of the bat against the ball, the ball against the leather glove, the thud of the batter's running feet. A few of the younger women were in the swings. We heard the chains creak and groan as the young men pushed them high in the air.

It was a typical happy picnic scene—and yet it was odd too. I watched a man run to one of the cars and lift out a heavy case of beer. It made a loud crash as he let it down on one of the wooden tables, and the bottles tinkled against each other. In the grill the fresh wood made little crackling explosions. The bat whacked the ball; the swings creaked. All these common sounds stood out uncommonly in the sunny air.

Martha and I felt the strangeness of it at the same moment.

"They're mutes," she whispered.

Then I realized that among the several dozen people we had heard not one voice and, though they were smiling broadly, not one sound of laughter. It was sad and strange and somehow, it seemed to me, a very natural part of the day so far.

"Where should I drop you?" she said as we drove past the old Pierce Mill and up onto Connecticut Avenue.

"Anywhere that's convenient. I'll grab a cab."

"Nothing of the kind. Last year you took me where I wanted to go. Now I'll take you. Back to the station?"

"No. I'm through for the day. My car's parked on M near Connecticut, if that's not out of your way."

She shook her head. The sun slanted through the window and flashed on her silver bracelet.

"You know," I said, "I've been thinking. We've been talking this afternoon—but in a way we've been like mutes too. Not really saying anything. Just making signs."

"What is it we haven't said?"

"I haven't asked you why—if you've known all summer I was in Washington—you didn't get in touch with me before this."

"I didn't want to risk you're not being interested in hearing from me, not remembering me."

"It would scarcely take everyone nine introductions. Why didn't you?"

"I didn't really have any reason to until this—this sort of business proposition came up."

"Just to see me wasn't a reason?"

She took her eyes off the road and looked at me. Her glance was very dark and distant.

"Why, no," she said.

We didn't talk much after that. I remember, driving through Dupont Circle, one of us remarked how confusing it was to have the streetcars going around to the left instead of to the right with the rest of the traffic. When we passed the Mayflower a short tan-faced general with a chestful of ribbons was signaling a cab. Martha waved at him. "Hello, Bootsie darling," she called out.

When she turned off the avenue onto M Street I pointed to a dusty cream-colored Crosley with a battered canvas top.

"That's mine."

She steered the station wagon up beside it, and I got out. Since I'd owned the Crosley everyone seemed to think it necessary to make some crack about it, about how tall I was and how short it was, and so forth. Martha didn't say anything.

"Good-by and thanks," I said. "I'll see you tomorrow night."

As she drove away I noticed again the initials on the door, L.M.S. Lloyd M. Seabright.

4

I put the Crosley's top down for the ride home. I needed plenty of air to prepare me for entering my apartment. In Washington if you dial WE 1212 an operator will tell you the weather forecast, the relative humidity, and the ardent desire of the telephone company to secure your services. After my first week I found these pieces of information superfluous, especially the middle one. My four rooms functioned from the beginning like a Turkish bath, no less efficient and a lot more expensive than the professional establishments downtown.

I had sublet the place from a Mr. Pearse, a civil servant, a CAF-7, as he put it. His wife had walked out on him during an altercation over a gentleman (CAF-10) in the Bureau of the Budget. It seemed she had done this once before, and Mr. Pearse then, as now, moved in with a brother and rented the apartment. Due to his addiction to the cliché that a woman always changes her mind, he wouldn't give me a lease. I lived from week to week, dependent upon the whimsical love life of Mrs. P. Nor had the OPA treated itself to a look at the furniture before they set the ceiling, figuring, I presume, that a table is a table and a chair is a chair. They were mistaken. In Mr. Pearse's apartment a chair is a maroon plush "English lounge" with broken spring cushion and kapok like popcorn bursting from the seams.

Literally, there was in the place not one pleasing article upon which to rest one's eye except the photograph of my small son Stevie I had set on the dresser, Stevie grinning to show his two new enormous front teeth, his short springy hair glistening under the photographer's lights. But in spite of the dreariness of Mr. Pearse's possessions I did no complaining out loud. Memory was too sharp of that first week when I was reduced to considering a phone booth as a residence. If there is no other place, a phone booth doesn't seem improbable, especially those in the Statler, equipped with commodious tilt-back chairs.

Also, if I needed cheering up I could take heart from the several samples of Mr. Pearse's hobby that hung about the apartment. These were optimistic admonitions such as *Smile and the World Smiles with You* burned onto slabs of wood and decorated with scrolls and roses. One plaque suspended between the twin beds bore a quatrain entitled *Remembering,* and over the telephone table there was another, succinctly announcing: *Telephone.*

After I had taken a long shower and dressed and was running over in my mind a list of air-conditioned restaurants that sign *Telephone* caught my eye. I picked it up and dialed a number.

It took Lieutenant Commander Rudolph Jennings a long time to answer the phone. He had, he explained, been at a crucial point in the making of lobster Newburg. Rudy was a bachelor and a subscriber to *Gourmet Magazine,* modestly famous for the small parties he gave. But at the moment what interested me were the parties he went to. He had always "gotten around" when I knew him in Cleveland, and from his remarks the few times I'd seen him lately I gathered his social success in the Capital was just as accomplished.

"Come on over for dinner," he told me. "Bill Sommers is bringing a girl, and I've got a lieutenant j.g. with big blue eyes. Her father raises horses in Texas."

"Thanks," I said. "I can't make it tonight. As a matter of fact, I called up for a little information. Do you know a Mrs. Oscar Finchley?"

"Martha Finchley? I've met her a few times. Why?"

"Who is she, anyway?"

"She isn't anybody officially, if that's what you mean. She's a—a social queen. You know, a Washington hostess. She gives big parties and goes to big parties. Why?"

"She was on my broadcast today. I just wondered."

"A very attractive dame, don't you think? A bit too brainy for my taste. She's one of these *informed* women—quotes Walter Lippmann and the *Congressional Record* and all that. Now this j.g. I mentioned is more the down-to-earth type—an authority on Glanders and Farcy. Come on over and meet her."

"Have you ever been to one of those Finchley Sunday-night affairs, Rudy?"

"Captain Leeds took me once. She's got a big layout on S Street and she puts on a real show, let me tell you. The place was full of gold braid and striped pants. The talk is that she wields influence, as they call it, with some of her regular guests. I wouldn't know. Some big shots, some Supreme Court justices even, will go anywhere if it means good food and liquor."

"What's the matter with going there?"

"Nothing. It's just amazing to see all the 'names' she rakes in. After all, she's not even the McCoy socially. No real connections. Her husband was a department-store tycoon. He left her a barrel of money and she knows how to throw a party. That combination works as well as anything in this town. If you want some dope, though, you ought to read Enid Hoyt's column. She's a friend of Martha Finchley's and she's always running items about her."

"I wouldn't buy that stinking *Press-Telegram* to read my own obituary. Which reminds me—I don't think I'll be riding this Sunday. When I spend three bucks to get on a horse I don't want to pass out from sunstroke."

"Then I'll take my new cowgirl."

My giving up the ride was the only way he'd get to take her on a Sunday. In Washington that summer there were waiting lists for horses as for everything else.

After we'd said good-by the thought of his lobster made me hungry and sorry for a moment that I hadn't accepted his invitation to dinner. But I was tired and, in a way, too excited to concentrate on the kind of conversation one always made at Rudy's, the skipping-stone inanities that he had so much success with at parties. I decided to eat out of my own store of cans and then drive over to F Street and hunt up a relaxing air-conditioned movie. But first of all I hurried down to the lobby and bought a *Press-Telegram*.

It wasn't hard to find Enid Hoyt's column. She had a big spread on the society page with a banner across the top reading "Capital Carousel" and a little caricature of her on a bulging-eyed merry-go-round horse. She was a dark girl with bangs and a turned-up nose. The drawing made her look, as I discovered she wrote, horribly impish.

There was nothing in the column that day about Martha, but I had read every word of it anyway. Some of the items it contained were a story about a cocktail party at someone's estate in nearby Virginia; a play-by-play description of the ornithological millinery of the women guests; a discussion of the three varieties of debutantes (family and money, family, money); a nomination for the best, as Miss Hoyt wrote it, "buzom" in Washington. I forget the name of the lucky lady, but no doubt others were not so careless. There was also a verse about a liberal State Department undersecretary whose vocation was poetry. Its bad scansion was probably more insulting to him than its planned rudeness. There was a paragraph about how much the non-fraternization policy in Austria was worrying a certain archduke, and finally hints of minor domestic scandal in Old Georgetown, "tsk tsk."

Miss Hoyt's journalism was coy, and her tongue clicks peppered the column. The "Carousel's" over-all attitude seemed to be that it was revealing what makes the world go round. It was, however, a world which couldn't exist outside the columns of the *Press-Telegram,* where God knows anything could happen and where the nightmares of the owner were set down daily in ten-point type on the editorial page.

The whole thing had a kind of depressing fascination, like those articles you find in novelty stores, intricate full-masted schooners inside bottles, or Bibles as big as postage stamps. Obviously somebody cares enough to make those things—but why? That's what I wondered about Enid Hoyt's column.

F Street every night was like the main drag of a college town on Saturday. Everyone seemed young and eager-eyed; everyone was on the town, out to let off steam, to find adventure, to have fun. These were the people who could never have made Enid Hoyt's column, whose social life bloomed not in the drawing rooms in Massachusetts Park or the swank slums of Georgetown, but downtown on the streets in the bright public light of the movie marquees. These were the government girls who paraded arm in arm and four abreast past the elegant windows of Garfinckle's, past the waffle shops and shoe shops and ten-cent stores and jewelry shops. These were the hundreds of soldiers and sailors in from nearby camps and bases who stood in little groups outside drugstores and servicemen's centers and stared at the bare legs and thin cotton dresses of the government girls and whistled and wondered what to do next. These were all the anonymous workers of Washington who surged and eddied into the smoky neon-lighted bars and the white-tiled cafeterias, who stood three-deep at drugstore counters, and who ended up like everyone else, in long lines waiting to be sucked up bit by bit into the maw of the movie houses.

I walked almost the entire length of the street to find a movie without a Standing Room Only sign. Finally I came to one that showed second runs. There was no line outside. I stopped before the display of glossy stills to see what was playing, and suddenly I gaped at one of the photographs. It was the same girl all right, the same arch look and dewy blond beauty of the abandoned pin-up in that farmhouse near Nancy. For the second time that day the memory of it made my heart pound. I bought a ticket and went inside.

I don't know yet what the title of that movie was, but no title could have described it. It seemed to be about a flier who thought this blond girl was going to be a man because her name was Ivy, which he read as I.V. They went on a bond tour together, and Ivy woke up one night to find the flier taking off his pants in her bedroom, a situation which didn't disturb her as much as it did two girls sitting next to me. A succession of gasps, groans, giggles, and screeches came out of the darkness to my right. When after some furious dialogue the flier perceived the hotel clerk's mistake (I.V. for Ivy again) I heard a long sigh of relief and a limp arm bumped mine as my neighbor relaxed.

Later it turned out that the flier was the victim of an incurable disease. Ivy married him. (Great tenseness to my right.) Somewhere along here Ivy wore a black evening gown and looked out of the screen at us from under her raised eyebrows.

"Who's that in the black dress over there?" Martha had asked, looking across the room at the pin-up on the wall.

"An ancestor," I suggested. "Some Frenchman's great-great grandmother."

"Seriously, this pin-up business puzzles me. Don't these beautiful, glamorous, unattainable girls make the boys dissatisfied with the ones they can get?"

"The boys tell me they aren't unattainable if one's imagination is good enough. One can give anyone's face and name to the girl one is making love to."

"Yes." She leaned back and glanced at me through the spiraling cigarette smoke. "I suppose one can."

"But afterward one feels foolish and cheated."

"The way you're feeling now?"

I turned to her and blinked in astonishment. It didn't go with her cool superiority, her flip assurance.

"There's a nice little girl back home, isn't there?" She asked with a sly, triumphant smile.

"There isn't anything back home. There isn't any home. There's only you and now."

"That's a sweet speech." She took my hand. "I'm older than you, but somehow you don't bring out my maternal instincts at all. Not at all."

She kissed me and proved what she'd said.

5

I don't recall the rest of the picture very well. The flier died, and the snifflings at my right reached a mounting intensity as the scenarists had written four endings to the film: a shot of Ivy toasting her dead husband, a shot of Ivy's upturned face as an airplane is heard overhead, a close-up of Ivy's face as her husband's voice speaks miraculously from the plane, a shot of sunlight through clouds as the sound track picks up the mounting voices of a presumably angelic chorus.

When the house lights went up for a short intermission I examined the two mourners at my side. The nearest one blew her nose into a piece of Kleenex, then looked at me and smiled. She had dimples and a pert, pretty face framed in a circle of yellow curls.

"I'm a sucker for sad pictures," she volunteered. "I cry like hell at the movies."

"I can see that," I answered.

Her companion, an ugly duckling with a startled expression, leaned over to see what was going on, but our conversation was ended, for the lights went down again and the screen announced we would now be entertained by Manny Kelvin at the organ. From the ceiling a rosy spot shone down on Mr. Kelvin's slick hair and the rows of keys in front of him. "Come on now, everybody," the screen entreated, "let's forget all our troubles and sing. Let's chase those blues away. Sing out, everyone." Then the lyrics appeared.

> *"Lost in the dark, left without a dream*
> *Lost in the unfolding of a tale without a*
> *   scheme—"*

The voices of the audience filled the theater; faces front, eyes on the screen, they sang to their private destinies.

The girl beside me pleaded in a wistful soprano:

> *"Caught in the careening of a fate that has no*
> *   meaning*
> *I could make the ending right*
> *If I had someone to turn to in the night."*

Gradually her voice lost its anonymity and became loud and clear. She knew exactly how to take a torch song and wind it around the heart. When it was over there was a smattering of applause around us, and some people in the row ahead turned to look at her.

"You sing as well as you cry," I told her.

"I can do that one in my sleep. I must've sung it a thousand times overseas."

"Were you a Wac?"

"Do I look like a Wac?" she demanded. "Not me. I was with the USO." Her glance dropped to my buttonhole and found what it was seeking. "Did you get overseas?" she asked. "To Italy, by any chance?"

The audience was now chanting some kind of paean to Rhode Island. "Little Rhode Island, I think you're great, smallest of the forty-eight," or words to that effect.

"I was in England," I told her, "later in France."

"Get to Paris?"

"Sure."

The Rhode Island song ended with loud whistles from a few lonesome natives.

"Gee," she said. "We were supposed to go to Paris, but our act broke up and we had to join up with another one that stayed in Italy. Our m.c. drowned himself"—her mouth tightened—"the dope!"

She sang the next song and the next, but I wasn't listening. I was trying to figure out how I could talk to her outside where we could really talk. It was a long shot, but it was worth a follow-up. Or maybe it wasn't a long shot. How many people serving in the USO drown themselves? How many do it in Italy? On the other hand, what difference did it make if she had known Harvey Benson? Who cared about her version of his suicide, which (if it was his), it was plain, she considered a personal inconvenience? But the swift vision I had had of Harvey's body floating in the water returned and with it my disbelief and depression of the morning. I was ashamed that seeing Martha had chased all thoughts of Harvey out of my mind until now.

Manny Kelvin's efforts at exorcising our blues were over. The spotlight faded, but before I had a chance to speak the two girls beside me got up and left. I followed them out to a mirror in the lobby where they stopped to fuss with their hair.

"Excuse me," I began.

The dimpled one looked up, surprised, at my reflection above her own. I was rather surprised myself when I saw the welcome in her eyes. One never knows what he really looks like to other people. I thought of myself as a tall lanky guy, but though I shaved my face every day I wouldn't know how to describe it.

"Am I beautiful?" I'd asked the nurse when they took the bandages off me in the hospital. It was Lieutenant

Wentworth, the serious one, the one who didn't understand when we wisecracked, who looked bewildered from
one of us to the other, like a spectator at a tennis match.

"Men aren't beautiful," she corrected me, and then with
more conscientiousness than I really wanted she added, "I
think you're interesting-looking. Your face has nice twists
and quirks."

When she had moved on to the other end of the ward
I looked in my shaving mirror, noticing the lines around
my eyes and across my forehead and the gaunt look to my
mended jaw, and I thought, whatever it had been before
the war, it was no kid's face now. I remember lying there
feeling rotten because I was an old man and had no job
and no home of my own, and even Stevie seemed more
Caroline's than mine. All I had were twists and quirks.

Now in the lobby mirror these were enough, at any
rate, to win the approval of the little singer.

"Yes?" she said, turning around.

"I was wondering," I began again, and then I put the
question about Harvey aside because I could see now there
was all the time in the world for that and I didn't want to
flatten her expectations. She was really a cute little girl.
Her friend's eyes were rabbit-startled in her sallow face.

"I enjoyed your singing," I said. "I was wondering if
you and your friend would join me for a drink."

"Sounds all right to me," she answered promptly. "I
could use something tall and cold. How about you, Geraldine?"

"I—I don't know. I—I have a headache—" Geraldine
protested weakly.

"Then a drink will fix you up fine." The pretty one
smiled at me. "My name's Gloria Hart. That's my professional name. This is my cousin, Geraldine Hudock."

I introduced myself and we shook hands.

"Have you girls any preferences about where to go?" I asked.

Gloria gave me a sizing-up look. I must have passed some kind of economic test or possibly she just didn't care.

"I adore the Shoreham," she said, "but of course it's rather far from here."

I told them where my car was parked and if they didn't mind walking to the lot we could easily drive up to the Shoreham. Gloria agreed immediately. "You'll like it," she told Geraldine. "They have tables and an orchestra out on the terrace and colored lanterns. It's the most glamorous place in town," she announced with the languid assurance of one who had made the rounds.

On the way to the car we exchanged some elementary information. They were both from the Middle West, from a little town called Lester. Geraldine was a stenographer on civil service, CAF-3, she said, in the Navy Department. Gloria referred to herself as a private secretary.

"I got fed up with show business," she explained. "It's all in the breaks. That girl in the movie tonight. She was just a model until some Hollywood producer noticed her picture in a magazine."

"Robert Montgomery and Gene Kelly came into our office last week," Geraldine boasted. "I saw them."

"No one like that ever comes into our office," said Gloria. "My boss isn't in the right racket, I guess."

I thought that, whatever his racket, her boss couldn't be needing much letter writing. Here under the bright street lights I got a better look at her, and she didn't look like any secretary. She had too much make-up on, and those long red nails weren't preserved by hitting a type-writer. But maybe her boss needed another kind of private secretary. Secretary, as Enid Hoyt had written about debu-tante, is a word of many varieties.

When they saw the car the girls giggled and exclaimed over it as if it were something under a Christmas tree. Even Geraldine looked happier.

We squeezed in and I started up Connecticut Avenue. Gloria put her head back and sighed as the breeze blew in our faces.

"It's a lot more comfortable than a jeep," she said.

"By the way," I said, "before you went overseas were you in radio work?"

"No." She shook her head and glanced at me. She had been visibly impressed, before when I told her what I did. "I sure would like to be, though—"

"I was wondering if you had known a friend of mine, a radio news analyst who headed up a USO unit that went to Italy. His name was Harvey Benson." We were a tight fit in the Crosley, and when that convulsive shudder shot through her body it was like feeling it go through my own.

She said, "I never heard of him."

We stopped for a traffic light at Dupont Circle. As casually as I could I went on, "He's supposed to have committed suicide over there—but I can't believe he did."

With one swift gesture Gloria released the catch of the car door and the two of them got out.

"What's the matter? Say, what is this?" I asked loudly. But they were already half running around the corner. A sailor rocked on his heels and grinned at me from the curb.

"Maybe they don't like your kiddie car, bud!"

By the time the light changed and I turned into the circle they had disappeared.

That night it wasn't just the heat that kept me from sleeping. I lay in the bedroom, the shades and windows high, and I thought about Martha and how she'd said, "I'll be glad to answer any questions." And I lay there feeling wonderful because I'd see her the following night—Tuesday night on S Street. I thought about Caroline, how her flower face bobbed happily over bridge tables and roulette tables; how she looked in the morning, pale and pouting the minute she opened her eyes, and the filmy nightgowns she wore not to please me but, as I discovered soon enough, to please herself only. I worried for a long time, too, over our son Stevie, whom I hadn't known for half his six years. I thought, Next week I'll have him come to Washington for a visit before school opens. I'll take him sight-seeing, get acquainted with him. I worried about him living with my parents—good people with the best intentions in the world and all their intentions mistaken. I snapped on the light and looked at his picture and wished he didn't resemble Caroline so much. But hell, why not? Caroline was the beauty in the family. Caroline the play-game girl. What a time she must have had in Reno.

But all this was only preliminary to what was really bothering me—the two girls I'd picked up in the movie, the way they'd reacted when I mentioned Harvey Benson. The thought of them stuck like a barb in my brain, hurt when touched. Maybe because I knew I was going to have to do something about it. And I didn't know what and I didn't want to. What did it mean? Why had Harvey killed himself and why were the circumstances such that a girl who'd known him, been working with him (and I was positive she had), leaped right out of an automobile when his name was mentioned?

The vision I had had in the morning of Harvey's slender body floating in the lake returned, and suddenly I knew why I had seen him in a sweat shirt and shorts. Back in the incredibly long-ago days of our boyhood he had never gone into the high school pool. For some medical reason—I forget exactly what—he had been excused from swimming classes. When we were in the pool Harvey had to go out and trot around the athletic field. I remembered how he looked standing in the locker room, his legs so white and bony under the track shorts, and the half-wistful grin on his face while we taunted him for being a speed merchant. Harvey had never learned to swim.

If he had fallen into a lake in Italy he certainly had a good chance of drowning. But how had he come to fall in, and under what conditions that there had been no one to pull him out? The answer was that he jumped in, that he wanted to die. That was apparently the answer in the newspapers at the time it happened. It wasn't my answer. I didn't believe it. But what was I going to do about it?

I got up and wandered about the apartment and took a bottle of beer out of the icebox and drank it. Then I stood at the window for a long time. I could see the lights in the windows of the other apartments nearby, the white fluorescent gleam from the laboratories of the Bureau of Standards, the rows of street lamps along Connecticut Avenue, and the smaller lights in the houses on Reno Road.

I was thinking about the time fifteen years ago—it seemed like fifty—that Harvey Benson had won the history-prize trip to Washington. When he returned he gave an "oral report" to the class. He used the elaborate oratorical style affected by the school debating society, but his voice even then was the vital, vibrant voice that later was to establish his career in radio. I reminded myself that I'd never really been sightseeing in the Capital. I ought to go soon. When Stevie comes, maybe. Finally I went to bed and to sleep.

I dreamed I was in an airplane flying on a fine night over Washington. Below me lay the silvery Potomac and the beautiful snowflake design of the lighted city. I heard my own voice saying, "Lost in the dark," and someone answered, "I'm afraid my reactions are quite, quite, quite different."

Then I jumped and there was no sensation at all, just the silken white cloud of parachute hovering over me and a wonderful light, descending feeling. I fell for several minutes amid cool uprushing currents of air until I saw a white spire below, and next I was on a gentle slope of grass and the sun was shining and beside me was the Monument, glittering and tall. A stream of sight-seers was pouring out of the entrance. Suddenly a man rushed over to me and grasped my arm.

"Sir, I am taking an important poll," he said breathlessly. He shoved the microphone he was holding up to my mouth. "The question, sir, is why do you go on living? To put it plainly, why don't you kill yourself?"

I glared at him and snatched my arm away and sealed my lips together. He turned and ran to the others. He tore at their coats and jackets to hold them still before his microphone, but all of them pushed him aside and turned their heads and no one answered. Desperately he asked his question over and over, but the line of sight-seers made a big detour around him, as if they were avoiding a savage beast.

I woke up, the nerve in my cheek fluttering like a snared bird. It was raining hard outside, the curtains were flapping, and a cool breeze was blowing over me.

6

I stood in front of Martha's door promptly at eight-thirty on Tuesday evening. She lived in a luxurious town house typical of that neighborhood in the Capital. It was large and square, four stories high, set flush with the sidewalk, the garden, as usual, in the rear. The window frames were white, the walls red brick where they showed through the clinging, glistening vines spread over them. The house looked historic and solid and American. I recognized Martha's sense of the appropriate. If she had lived in Venice I'm sure it would have been in a doge's palace, with gondolas tied at the door. If in Alaska, the biggest, whitest igloo. Since she lived in Washington, this was obviously a home for her.

The door was heavy paneled wood painted a dark green with a wrought-iron lighted lantern hanging over it. The brass of its knocker (an eagle, rampant and arrogant) and its doorknob shone with a patina that comes from treatment each morning by muscle and polishing rag.

My ring was answered by a colored butler who said Mrs. Finchley was expecting me. He showed me upstairs into an immense drawing room, green-walled, two glowing oriental rugs covering its floor, and furnished with polished mahogany period pieces. I didn't know which period, but I was sure it was the right one for the house.

Above the fireplace, screened now by ivy trailing from the mantel, was a huge imitation-Dali portrait of Martha with a drawer jutting out of her chest and a fried egg over one ear. The four people sitting under it had turned their gaze in my direction, and Martha was moving serenely across the room toward me. She wore a simple black dress cut low at the throat, her hair pulled back from her face and coiled on her neck. She looked cool and uncluttered and beautiful.

"Alec," she said, "you're very prompt." Her reserve of yesterday afternoon had lessened. She pressed my arm warmly and guided me over to the others. When we reached the fireplace she said, "This is Alexander Pike. You've all heard him, now you can see him."

The two men rose. The two women looked at me with frank curiosity.

"Mrs. Seabright," Martha said, and I found my hand in the firm grasp of a bony gray-haired woman with black thick eyebrows and a determined smile. Three diamond bracelets jangled on her wrist as we shook hands. "And Miss Hoyt." I had already recognized Enid Hoyt. Like the caricature which topped her column, her features were just a bit out of whack, the nose too far turned up, the eyes too large, the chin too pointed, but I saw that she had the shapeliest and probably the longest legs in the world. They were encased in sheer nylon and crossed, the free foot swinging slightly in its black sandal. Miss Hoyt shook my hand with, I thought, an eagerness out of all proportion to the occasion.

The younger man, heavy-set and balding, jerked my hand briefly and gave me a suit-salesman's look of appraisal. When I heard his name, however, I knew he didn't sell suits. He sold articles to magazines. Hardly a week went by that some slick publication didn't announce: "The Truth about Capitol Hill," by Howard Linzell, "The Real

Truth about Capitol Hill," by Howard Linzell, "The Inside Story of Capitol Hill," by Howard Linzell, or as a variation, "What Really Happened behind the White House Door," by Howard Linzell. This article was sometimes published under the title, "Inside the Pentagon." As is to be expected of a young man who spent so much time on the inside of things, Mr. Linzell had a sallow complexion and permanently red-rimmed eyes.

The other man was, I learned later, just over fifty years old, but he didn't look it. He was huge and handsome with thick fair hair and the tight, fresh-looking skin of a man used to cold showers and massage. His smile exhibited square white teeth nicely set in his jaw. Like the characters in the whisky ads, he had a terrific air of distinction. This, I thought, is L.M.S. Lloyd M. Seabright, the white-haired boy.

"Alec," said Martha, "I want you to meet Lloyd Seabright."

He clasped my hand in his huge one and gave it a hearty shake.

The butler appeared then with a tray of glasses, and we sat drinking and talking for a few minutes. Miss Hoyt told me that she didn't like the idea of my switching to a once-a-week show when she enjoyed listening to me every day and where did I find those fascinating little people I interviewed? I said it was kind of her to assume I'd work out on their new show but, after all, this was just a tryout on both our parts, wasn't it? Linzell laughed and said he was sure they could use my professional touch, as I'd see when they played the records. Then Lloyd Seabright asked what we were waiting for, and Martha and he walked over to an enormous mahogany cabinet which turned but to be the latest-model radio-phonograph with as many dials as the dashboard of a C-54. There seemed to be some discussion as to which set of records to run, and while they were making up their minds Mrs. Seabright gave me another strained bright smile and said she'd heard my Victory Parade broadcast the other day.

"Lloyd had two good places for us right on the Capitol steps," she said, "but I can't stand heat and crowds. I preferred my chaise longue, a big scotch and soda, and your interesting impressions, Mr. Pike."

"It was the parade of everybody's boyhood dreams," I said. "I'm afraid I succumbed to all the rah-rah."

"But why not? There seems to be a hint of apology in what you just said, Mr. Pike. Why are people ashamed to be carried away by patriotism? I think love of country is one of the noblest emotions there is, don't you? When I see the Stars and Stripes or the Capitol dome or the uniform of the United States Army I get a lump in my throat and I'm not ashamed to admit it—"

"Those Navy dress whites are the most gorgeous uniforms in the world," sighed Enid Hoyt.

Linzell looked at my lapel. His own was empty. "Were you Navy?" he asked.

"Army."

"I—I missed out on that big show." He shook his head, and his lips tightened at the thought of such a tough break. "One of those damn-fool kid football injuries. I'd have given anything to—"

His words ended in the usual vague mumble. Given anything to do specifically what? I always wanted to ask those guys. When I'd first gotten back so many of them had thought it necessary to refer to the disasters of a youthful football game that I'd started making a private tally of what the sport had done to the manhood of America. Well, here's one more, I told myself.

"It's thrilling," Mrs. Seabright was saying, "to see those boys marching row on row, thousands of them, all so brave and straight and manly—"

"I thought you missed the parade, Alice," said Enid Hoyt.

"Well, I could imagine it, couldn't I? With Mr. Pike's help?" She gave Miss Hoyt a hostile stare.

"When I saw those boys," Linzell said, his lips tight at the tragic emotion of it, "I was damn glad the war was over."

"Is it?" Mrs. Seabright gave us all a meaningful glance. "Do you think all our enemies are dead, Howard? That's a rather naive way of thinking, isn't it, Mr. Pike?"

I said mildly that I hoped our enemies were down and out for a long time.

"But that's extremely naive," Mrs. Seabright complained. "By the way, what happened during your street interview? I heard some kind of a tussle just before Martha came on."

"Nothing much. Some roughneck."

"What was he trying to do?"

"He didn't get much of a chance to do or say anything. I cut him off pretty fast—"

"Then you don't allow free speech on your interviews? You believe in free speech, don't you, Mr. Pike?"

"I used to think I did. Now I honestly don't know."

"It's a dilemma," Linzell said. "It's a dilemma."

Just then a loud, enthusiastic voice from the phonograph exclaimed, "It's Sunday Night on S Street!" and we stopped talking to listen to the records.

"How would you like to be entertained in a famous Washington mansion?" the voice demanded reverently. In the background the sound effects simulated a party hubbub. "To move about in a galaxy of the great and near great, rub shoulders with people of affairs, people who are doing important things in the world today? How would you like to meet them in the spontaneous informal atmosphere of a gay supper party? Listen to their conversation?

Hear their opinions? The Finchley Stores invite you now to be among those present at the home of Mrs. Martha Finchley, celebrated and charming Washington hostess."

The sound effects grew louder. There was music and conversation and the clinking of glasses and dishes. Soft Southern voices of servants named and offered dishes from the buffet. The announcer's voice said, "Now let us step into the beautiful book-lined library where Mrs. Finchley is welcoming this evening's guest of honor, Justice Lionel Haylor."

Martha's voice came through the mike with just the right warmth and authority for a celebrated and charming Washington hostess. From then on she more or less acted as the master of ceremonies. Enid Hoyt, in a high girlish voice, made characteristically cute comments on the gowns and the glamour. Seabright was splendid. At one point there was a hot discussion between him and a visiting English economist about the Bretton Woods Conference in which Seabright showed expert knowledge of international finance.

When all the sides had been played Martha switched off the phonograph and looked at me. Everybody looked at me.

"Of course," she apologized, "it was only a dry run. These people knew they weren't on the air. They'd probably have made more effort if—"

"It was all right," I interrupted. "In fact, I am agreeably surprised. That doesn't mean it couldn't be a lot better, you know that. You wasted all kinds of opportunities. It's—it's too much like the *Chicago Round Table,* for instance. It needs drama—gimmicks."

"Gimmicks!" exclaimed Enid Hoyt. "That's cute."

"What?" asked Seabright.

"You know, Lloyd," Linzell explained. "Hickeys, things, tricks, attention getters, pep—"

"Well, gimmicks are just what we want you for," Martha told me. "We know the show needs vitality; it needs one person to pull it all together and keep it going. I feel it getting away from me all the time."

"The timing's bad, don't you think?" Seabright asked. "Martha doesn't seem to be able to handle the long-winded gaffers or to pull the good stuff out of the reluctant ones."

"We have several other records," Martha said, "if it will help you to hear them. We cut three complete half-hours."

"I want to hear them. Maybe tomorrow. But right now I have some suggestions. Now see what you think of this."

I outlined the ideas that had occurred to me for restyling the show, for giving it pace and variety. It was one of those times when my mind clicked along fast and unimpeded, and the others caught my enthusiasm. Martha beamed at me like a lady magician who had just produced the rabbit. Linzell made some good publicity-wise recommendations. Miss Hoyt crossed and uncrossed her long legs and said she was delighted with everything. Mrs. Seabright refilled her glass two or three times and sat silently gazing at me over its rim. Seabright himself was very cautious. Several times he asked me to repeat what I had said, but after he got it straight he usually agreed. Soon I realized that I was speaking mainly to him. There seemed to be a feeling in the room that he, not Martha, was the one most concerned. I noticed how very much at home he was, how he went directly to the right drawer for the carton of cigarettes when we needed them, how he, not Martha, rang for more ice. I got a glimmer of the reason why Mrs. Seabright had seemed to channel her emotions toward marching soldier boys.

And then when the stocky white-haired man appeared at the door it was Seabright first and Martha second who sprang up and hurried to greet the newcomer. The white-haired man had fat cheeks and round, apprehensive blue eyes that circled the room and came to a halt on me. I heard the others say, "Hello, Governor," and then Seabright brought him over and said, "Governor, I want you to meet Mr. Pike. Governor Colston."

I remembered him then. He'd aged a lot since his picture had been in *Time* a few years ago in connection with some party-machine scandal in his state. His handshake was bone-crushing and automatic.

"Well, sir," he said, "how are things going? I hear you're an expert. Now, as an expert, what do you think of the lady's little project?"

"It's going to do the work, Governor," Linzell answered for me. "Mr. Pike is a real find. Were extremely encouraged."

"By God, that's wonderful!" The governor took the glass that Martha brought him. "Here's to—what do they call it, Mr. Pike? Hooper rating? Here's to your Hooper rating!"

"Where's Sidney?" Seabright asked.

"I had to take him home. He was all worn out after the dinner and the speeches. I'm worried about him; he seems to be fading away since his wife died."

"What can you expect at his age?" asked Enid Hoyt.

"All the same, I'm worried. He looks like a very sick man." The governor wagged his head. "I'm afraid we don't have too much time, Lloyd."

Seabright shrugged. "We'll do the best we can with the time we have."

He and Martha began to tell the governor about my ideas for reworking the show. Mrs. Seabright filled her glass again and sipped away at it silently in a corner. I walked over and sat down on the couch next to Enid Hoyt. "What did the governor mean?" I asked her. "They haven't much time for what?"

"For gimmicks." Miss Hoyt grinned at me. "They need a lot of gimmicks for Lloyd. He's supposed to get the senatorial appointment when Sidney Witherell resigns."

"Oh, they were talking about *that* Sidney!"

"Sidney's not well. He's going to resign in six months or so. I don't know all the details, but the governor is obligated to Martha and Lloyd, and he's doing the only civilized thing there is to do—he's appointing Lloyd. You know—politics." She grinned again. "Of course this program is all a build-up for Lloyd, but I don't care, I think it's going to be loads of fun."

A few minutes later the butler rolled in a cart with a cold turkey on it and a silver coffeepot. We ate and discussed the show some more, and now that I had the key from Enid Hoyt I could translate much of the conversation I'd not have understood so well otherwise. I gathered that Linzell was handling public relations for Seabright and that he was in the midst of a big campaign to play down Seabright's socialite country-gentleman background and get him press attention as a valuable wartime government servant. He mentioned that he had written several articles on Seabright which were to appear in magazines soon. The governor was anxious, I could tell, to be friendly to Seabright, but he seemed worried as to how the appointment would go down at home. He kept mentioning "the boys" and keeping "the boys happy" and "making everything all right with the boys." I didn't know he meant veterans, not politicians, until he clapped me on the shoulder and called me "you boys" and told me that nothing was too good for us boys.

After a while the governor said that Washington ran him ragged and he'd be glad to get back to the sticks tomorrow and as he had to catch an early plane he'd like to be excused. Then everyone said it was time to go and we all went down into the large entrance hall and were given

our hats and shook hands all around and said we were glad
to have met.

"What time can you come to work tomorrow?" Martha
asked me.

I said I'd be over in the early afternoon. Linzell and
Seabright agreed to drop in around cocktail time to offer
their services. The governor told us to keep in touch and
that he'd be glued to the radio next Sunday. Then we all
left the house and the big green door shut behind us.

"Oh, what a cute little car!" exclaimed Miss Hoyt when
she saw the Crosley.

"What do you tank it up with?" asked Linzell. "Carna-
tion milk?"

I drove slowly up Massachusetts Avenue, down R Street,
up Connecticut, and finally back along S. There was a car
across the street from Martha's home which hadn't been
there before. An old but shining Cadillac convertible with
a New York license plate. I left the Crosley behind it and
walked up to the door. The lantern above it was still on,
and so were the lamps in the second-floor windows. As I
started to press the bell I felt that nerve jigging away in
my cheek. Oh, what the hell am I doing here? I thought. If
she wanted to see me alone she'd have indicated it. Better
go home to Mr. Pearse's apartment, to his electric fan and
his wooden homilies and my own solitude. But whether
she wanted to see me or not wasn't the point. I looked
into the little staring brass eye of the bell. I wanted to
see her. I was going to see her. Nothing ventured, nothing
gained, et cetera. I'll have to tell that one to Mr. Pearse,
I thought. I'll have to get him to burn that one on wood
for me.

I turned away from the door and walked across the
grass to the back of the house. In the garden the last of
the summer flowers stood silhouetted in the moonlight,

like soldiers watching me, the advance patrol. I stepped up onto the terrace. The long doors into a sitting room were open, and a table light sent a small glow through the room, catching on the cigarette boxes, on the gold lettering of the book covers. I eased myself into a low bamboo chaise longue and waited.

Instantly I was aware that someone else was on the terrace with me. A few feet away I saw the glowing tip of a cigarette move through the air and, beyond it, the denser darkness of a body's bulk. A chair creaked gently, and then a voice, melodious and foreign, said, "This night is so beautiful it looks phony, you know—like a stage-set waiting for the actors and the dialogue."

"All right," I agreed, "shall we speak a few lines?"

"I might play the jealous suitor, but who are you?"

"The business acquaintance."

"Ah, but this is no hour for business," the voice reproached me. "I really should boot you out of here since I have—what do you call it?—seniority. However"—he sighed, and the cigarette made a little comet's path into the bushes—"I am a very relaxed type of personality, so I say welcome."

"Thank you," I answered coldly.

Just then Martha came through the door carrying a tray and two tinkling glasses. I heard her set it down, and then she walked to the edge of the terrace and stood looking out into the garden. The moonlight glanced along her dress.

"We need another glass, my darling," said the voice. "Tonight we are three."

I stood up. "Hello," I said, and then rather unnecessarily, "I came back."

She whirled around. "This is a surprise! Have you two gentlemen met? Carlos, this is Mr. Pike. Remember, I was telling you about him? He's going to m.c. our show. Alec, this is Mr. San Martin."

The stranger rose from his chair and our hands groped and met. We were facing each other in the darkness like blind men, but I could tell that he was much shorter than I and his hand felt smooth and soft. Suddenly I placed his accent.

Martha was saying, "I'll go fix another drink."

"Don't bother," I began.

"Of course I will. And it's no bother. I'm delighted, Alec."

When she had gone Mr. San Martin said, "She is delighted too. Nothing pleases that kind of female more than the—storming of the fort."

I laughed. "That's a rather elaborate description for a hike through a garden—"

"But that is the way she will interpret it, my dear Mr. Pike. She will find it flattering even if it is inconvenient."

"I trust it's not inconvenient."

"It is. But we shall make the best of it, you know." A match flared for an instant as he held it sipped to a fresh cigarette. Before the flicker of light went out I saw his face, fleshy and handsome, with large bright black eyes and a thin black line of mustache. "So you are the radio genius."

"You are the friend from Buenos Aires."

"Is that how she calls me? It has been a long time since I have come from Buenos Aires. I have come from everywhere else since, it seems to me. My business—antiques, art gallery—took me everywhere before the war."

"Europe, I suppose?"

"Yes. Europe was a treasure house for me. Now I am afraid there is nothing left. Everything destroyed."

"Have you ever been to Italy, Mr. San Martin?"

"Oh yes, yes. I have many friends there. Italy is a most lovely country. Do you know Italy?"

"No. I— What made me think of it is some bad news I got recently. I heard a friend of mine killed himself over there."

"Suicide!" Mr. San Martin groaned. "That is the refuge of fools." And while he was giving all the reasons why he strongly disapproved of cutting life short Martha came back with my drink.

"How did you two get onto such a morbid subject?" she asked.

I told her how I'd heard about Benson's death the other day just before I ran into her.

"What did you say the name was?" asked Mr. San Martin. "Harvey Benson?"

"That's right. Have you ever heard of him?"

"Of course," Martha said. "I remember. He was a news analyst. I think he covered Washington for one of the networks a few years ago. I think I even met him once."

"See, my friends," interrupted Mr. San Martin, "see what a small world it is!"

"Why did he kill himself?" Martha asked me.

"That's what I'm curious about," I told her, "and I intend to do some investigating. When I knew him"—I turned to Mr. San Martin—"he was neither a fool nor a man in need of a refuge."

"Ah?" said Mr. San Martin. "And should you find out the motives for your friend's self-inflicted death, what would you do then?"

"There is nothing to do, is there?" I asked. "Except to understand?" I drained my glass. "This has been very pleasant," I said, "but I must be going."

Martha made no protest. "I'll walk out to your car with you," she said. "Excuse me a minute, Carlos."

I bade Mr. San Martin good night, and we went through the garden and across the street.

"I didn't mean to intrude," I told Martha.

"You didn't."

"As a matter of fact, I came back because I realized there were a couple of important questions I hadn't asked you. One is concerning the delicate subject of salary."

"And the other?"

"If the show is, as I know now, part of a publicity build-up for Lloyd Seabright, what happens when Seabright gets what he's after and no longer needs the build-up? Does the show close?"

"Of course not. I'm terribly excited about it. If it takes we'll go right on with it as long as we can, no matter what Lloyd does."

I had sat down behind the wheel and she was standing beside the car door looking down at me. I could smell the faint fresh scent she used and see her face mobile and mysterious in the glow of the street light.

"Martha," I said, "I didn't really come to ask questions. I came back to be with you. Go and send your South American friend away and—"

"As for the salary," she interrupted, "would five hundred a week be agreeable?"

I turned the key and started the motor. "Quite agreeable, thanks."

I drove on down the street, and when I looked into the rear-view mirror she had gone. Five hundred a week, I said to myself. That should have been one of the glad moments of my life. But it wasn't.

7

It didn't take much figuring to figure out the spot in the Navy Department where Miss Geraldine Hudock, one of my vanishing guests of the other night, was employed. When the movie stars she had mentioned got to town they were most likely, I thought, to be handled by the Office of Public Information. At any rate, it was a simple matter to think up an excuse to go over there and look for her—a matter which I took action on the next day after my noon broadcast.

Constitution Avenue was baking in the midday sun. The heat waves rising from the pavement distorted the long four-storied Navy Building—like looking at it under water but a lot less refreshing. I was glad to escape into the air-conditioned corridors of the Zero wing which, a clerk assured me, was the place to find Lieutenant Charles Shaver of the Office of Public Information.

I looked into all the rooms on the Constitution Avenue side with no success. At the door to the corner office I ran into a Wave seaman second class carrying a pile of folders.

"Who's in there?" I asked her.

"The admiral, sir."

I skipped the corner office. About six doors down on the Seventeenth Street side I found a small white card tacked at eye level. It read:

Lt. Charles P. Shaver
Press Section

Inside the room were six green steel desks and a couple of bookcases. And there at the very first desk, bent over a clacking typewriter, sat Miss. Hudock. Most of the other places were occupied by Waves, and in the rear near the window was Lieutenant Shaver. I had met him a couple of times at Rudy's apartment, and fortunately he remembered me.

"Why, hello, Alec!" He rose and held out his hand. "What are you doing on deck?"

The Waves looked up and so did Miss Hudock. I bestowed upon the latter an enormous smile and went over to the lieutenant. My business with him didn't take long. I wanted, I announced eagerly, a celebrity for a broadcast the following week. The lieutenant promised to give me special attention. Maybe, he said, maybe he could even get me Douglas Fairbanks, Jr.! He'd work on it.

"I wish you'd stopped in earlier," he told me. "We could have had lunch. As it is, I'm due at a CNO meeting right now."

"Don't let me keep you. Perhaps next week we can—" But he was out of the door before I'd finished. CNO, whatever it was, was plenty important. I walked over to Miss Hudock's desk and drew up a chair.

"And how are you today?"

"I'm all right." She gave me a defiant stare through her rimless glasses, and her bony face reddened.

"And how is your cousin, Miss Hart?"

"She's all right."

Suddenly I noticed a lack of talk and activity in the room. There was no sound save the hum of the air-conditioner in the corner. I could tell by Miss Hudock's rabbit stares at something behind me that the Waves had their eyes on us and were listening. I decided to make it easy for them.

"I came over especially to see if you'd go to lunch with me, Miss Hudock," I announced in a booming voice.

Her eyes snapped wide open as they met mine.

She started to shake her head. Then her glance darted around the room once more. Suddenly she said, "Why, yes, I will. I'd just love to." She consulted her wrist watch. "I have to be back by 1400. Excuse me just a minute." She took a white purse out of her desk and fled from the room. In the hall she collided with a Wave officer just coming in.

"My God"—the officer paused to catch her breath—"what's Hudock in such a dither about?"

"She's got a lunch date," whispered a sweet spiteful voice behind me.

"With a man! Who's the fall guy?"

I heard their muffled laughter and then the self-conscious back-to-business bustle. Woman's inhumanity to woman. However, maybe I was a fall guy in a quite different way. Miss Hudock and her cousin had hurried out of my car for a very good reason the other night—a reason I might be better off not inquiring about. My years in the Army had left me with acute allergy to entanglement and trouble. All I really wanted out of peacetime was some work I enjoyed doing and a few uncomplicated human relationships. Me and Martha—now that could be something "basic" if she'd only co-operate.

Miss Hudock returned in fresh lipstick and a white beanie and we set out for lunch. Contrary to my feelings a quarter hour before, it was rather a relief to escape from that stronghold of maidens in uniform. I put my hand gallantly under Miss Hudock's elbow and guided her toward New York Avenue.

"How about the Allies Inn," I asked her, "since you haven't a lot of time?"

She nodded primly. She kept her head down and seemed to be concentrating on keeping in step with me.

"Quite a bunch of girls you work with," I began experimentally.

"I hate them. They hate me. I'll be glad when they're gone."

"What's the trouble?"

"Oh, they're mad at anyone who isn't in uniform and who's getting paid more than they are. They think they're so noble, as if they joined the Navy to save the world! If it wasn't for Lieutenant Shaver I'd asked to be transferred." She looked up at me. "Do you know him well?"

"Not very well. I've met him a couple of times before."

"He's nice to me," she said. "He's human." Her face relaxed into a musing smile. "He says he's going to help me get a CAF-4."

When we got to the Allies Inn we joined the cafeteria line behind a stocky dark man.

"That's Baldwin Cole," Miss Hudock whispered. She glanced eagerly around the room. "I've heard lots of people from the State Department eat here too," she said. "I don't recognize anybody though."

"Do you come here much?"

"No. It's—it's too much for my budget." I remembered the girl clerk I had seen in a Treasury Department office one time when I was setting up my microphone for a broadcast. She had been absorbed in some figures on a pad all the time I was in the room, and when I threaded my wire behind her desk I saw it was a list of expenditures. "Friday," it said, and, then underneath, "cigarettes 17 cents, lunch 25 cents. . . ."

I tried to coax Missy Hudock into having the calves' liver and bacon, but she settled on a fruit salad. When we came to the ice-cream counter I asked for a scoop on my apple pie.

"One dessert to a customer, sir," the attendant informed me.

"Vanilla ice cream, please," said Miss Hudock. She put the dish on her tray and winked at me. It was such a pathetic gesture on her plain, unhappy little face—but it meant we had a bond between us now. We were fellow conspirators against the Allies Inn.

We sat down at one of the scrubbed wooden tables in the patio and began to eat.

After a few minutes of casual talk I said: "What in the world happened the other night? Why did you girls rush off like that? I really was going to take you to the Shoreham, you know. I hope you don't think that—"

"Oh no." She looked at me solemnly, "I didn't think anything. It was the first time I'd ever been—well—picked up—but I didn't think anything like that!"

"Then what was the matter?"

"Oh, it's my cousin Gloria. I never know what she's going to do. She's been acting funny since she's come back from overseas. She's been acting like she's shell-shocked." Miss Hudock laughed faintly.

"How do you mean?"

"Oh, she's nervous all the time. I guess she doesn't like her job. I guess she'd rather be back on the stage."

"Who does she work for?"

Miss Hudock's mouth was filled with grapefruit sections. She shrugged. It seemed impossible that she didn't know, but I decided not to press her at the moment.

"What puzzled me," I went on, "is that she didn't mind my talking to the two of you at all—not at first. She seemed happy to get my invitation."

"Oh, she loves to go places. She'd like to be taken out every night in the week. She complains that it's so hard to meet people in Washington, but she won't try my way."

"What way is that, Miss Hudock?"

"Oh, I don't usually talk about it." She stared down at her plate. "It's kind of silly, I guess. I know it's silly and I don't really take it seriously, but"—she glanced hesitantly up at me—"it's the only way I know. I go on tours—sight-seeing tours around Washington. You know how they are—busses and a guide. It takes all afternoon and—well, you get to talk to people that way—you get sort of acquainted. Trouble is, the people are mostly from out of town. But once, walking up to the top of the Washington Monument, I got to talking to a young man who worked here, and we were friends until he was drafted. I invited him to my state party."

"State party?"

"They have parties down here for all the people from a certain state—there's dancing and refreshments and you meet the people from your state. Our party was wonderful. Martha Finchley came with one of the congressmen."

"Who?"

"Martha Finchley. She's a very famous woman down here—a rich society woman. She gives absolutely fabulous parties at her house on S Street. Anyway, I got to shake hands with her and I'll never forget what she said. She said, 'I hope we daughters of the finest state in the union get together more often.' That was about four years ago. She's never come to any of the other parties since—but of course a woman like that is terribly busy."

She slid her vanilla ice cream off the plate and onto my apple pie. I ate it and thought about that old saying Mr. San Martin had been so excited about last night—what a small world it is. I considered asking Miss Hudock outright if she knew of or had heard anything about Harvey Benson, but I was afraid of scaring her away just as she was breaking down and getting confidential. The chances were that she could tell me nothing anyway. It was the other one, Gloria, that I had to see.

When we had finished lunch we walked back to the Navy Building.

"Well, Miss Hudock," I said, "it wasn't so bad—having lunch with me—was it?"

She smiled and blushed. I noticed for the first time what nice eyes she had, blue, marked off by thick black lashes. If only she didn't have to wear glasses. If only she didn't hold her body as if she were expecting to be tackled and thrown at any minute.

"How about letting me complete my invitation of the other night?" I asked. "How about letting me take you and your cousin to the Shoreham Friday evening?"

"Oh, Gloria couldn't go, I'm sure. I'm sure she has a date."

"Why don't you tell her to break it? Tell her I'm not so bad after all."

"It isn't that. But Gloria has a steady date on Fridays."

"How about Saturday?"

"Saturday too."

"O.K. You and I will go then. I'll pick you up Saturday at seven." I reached in my pocket for a pencil. "Just let me write down the—"

Her blue eyes seemed to retreat behind her glasses. She twisted her purse in her hands. "I'd better meet you there, I think. I think it would be better if I met you."

"Just as you say. In the lobby at seven?"

She nodded and ran up the steps and into the building. All right, I thought, there wasn't any hurry. Maybe I didn't know where they lived yet—but I'd find out Saturday evening. I'd use Lieutenant Shaver's technique on Miss Hudock, and eventually I'd get to her cousin Gloria. Miss H., I told myself, was a pushover for plain human decency.

I spent the rest of the afternoon on S Street working on Sunday's show. At four o'clock Seabright and Linzell stopped in for a drink, and we talked about some more and found them very pleased with what we had done.

When they had left I said to Martha, "Come on out to dinner with me. We'll go down to the New England Oyster Bar and eat lobsters out on the balcony and watch the sun set behind the Jefferson Memorial."

"Oh, I'm so sorry," said Martha, "but there's a small dinner party tonight at the French Embassy—"

8

The next afternoon I paid a call on my employer, Mr. Ralph H. Logan of the Logan Jewelry Company. His office was on E Street in the same building as his main store. As usual, several dozen people stood looking into the windows where countless glittering articles were displayed in boxes, satin-lined and hinged on top like little coffins. The corner window, however, really caught my eye. It was a decided departure for Logan's, empty save for a swishy drape of pink satin upon which in magnificent isolation gleamed two rings. At one side was an artfully lettered card:

Seal your happiness forever with
Logan's Summer Romance Special
Engagement-Wedding Ring Combination
$327.99 plus tax

In the bottom corner was reassuring advice to those Washington lovers who had had a wow of a summer but not three hundred dollars: "Ask about our time-payment plan."

I entered the building and took an elevator to the sixth floor. The receptionist in the outer office knew me, the manager in the inner office knew me, the private secretary in the private secretary's office knew me. I journeyed unimpeded to the English-oak door of the inner sanctum and I was ushered in.

About thirty feet away from me, crouched over a massive desk, his back to a row of neo-Gothic leaded-glass windows, was Mr. Logan. He was a short man, exceedingly overweight, with the jolly wreathlike smile of a Santa Claus and a similar gift psychology (you buy 'em—we deliver 'em). He had about him always a faint odor of a shaving lotion of a brand especially concocted for him and said to be reeking of heather and leather. It didn't go well with the seventeenth-century English atmosphere of the office decor.

"Oh, it's you, my boy." He made an expansive gesture. "Come in and close the door." I marched over the thirty feet of oyster-white carpeting and shook his hand.

"Sit down, my boy. Have a cigar?"

"No, thank you," I said. "I'll only be a minute. I've come to tell you something—"

"So?" he asked. "Well, it will take more than a minute for me to tell you something." He laughed loudly. "So sit down."

I eased myself into an antique red leather chair. Mr. Logan put down the fountain pen he was holding and pushed aside a white paper covered with his handwriting. Since he personally wrote all the ads for his company, I took it he was working over a new one. His eyes followed mine to the paper and then he said, "Say, you ought to be able to help me. You're a veteran."

He leaned back in his chair, his feet, in immaculate brown-and-white shoes, swinging clear of the floor. "I'm trying to get out a letter," he said, "a letter to all the boys who'll be coming back home. Want to remind them that Logan's is still on the map—you know what I mean. Now they're through with the battle of the Pacific, they got the battle of the sexes on their hands." He laughed uproariously.

"They're going to need wedding rings, my boy, and wedding rings is what Logan's has got to sell. Now tell me what you think of this."

He picked up the white paper. "We'll have our letter-head across the top, see, and then in capital letters three times we'll put WELCOME HOME. Now listen to this." He began to read: "'H'ya, fella, that's all I want to keep saying, and believe me, it's straight from the heart. I know you're busy seeing all your old friends, so I won't take much of your time. All I want to do is remind you that Logan's, the Capital's greatest jewelry store, is still here eager and ready to serve you. The job you did, fella, enti-tles you to the very best we can offer in merchandise and in credit. If you are looking for a ring for some partic-ular someone, remember you are more than welcome at Logan's. Before you carry her over the threshold of that little cottage of your dreams, be sure to slip one of Logan's diamond wedding bands on that slender finger. Come on in, fella, and get acquainted with us again.'" He tossed the letter back on his desk and exhaled heavily. "Well, what do you think of it, my boy?"

"I don't know," I said. "If the fellas wait till they can buy a cottage before they buy a ring, they'll be waiting ten years by the lowest FHA estimate."

"I could change it to cozy apartment."

"It might make them mad. There aren't any apartments either."

"Then how's this? 'Before you take her into your hun-gry arms, be sure to slip one of Logan's—' et cetera."

"It's kind of mid-Victorian, isn't it? Your suggesting that they can't neck a girl without marrying her?"

"The fellas won't like that, huh? How's this? 'Before you take her in your hungry arms, *why not* slip one of Logan's—'; et cetera. No harm in a simple question, is there?"

"Not exactly," I said.

He put a cigar in his mouth and twisted off the tip of it. His confidential creative mood was over. He scowled. "Well, now I have a bone to pick with you, my boy. That broadcast last Friday, that black sailor boy. No soap, Alec."

"What do you mean?"

"Now I know you're from up North and you people simply don't understand what the feeling's like down here, but I ain't going to get in an argument. I'm telling you. No soap."

"I still don't get it."

"My God!" He rolled his eyes at the oak-beamed ceiling. "I'm saying you cannot encourage a colored fella to talk the way that one did over the radio. Not in this town, you can't."

"This is the Capital of the United States."

"And the Capital of the United States happens to be a Southern town, Alec."

"But he didn't say anything that wasn't true. If they wouldn't let him into a movie downtown so he could have a place to sit till traintime, I think he should say what he thinks about that. I thought it was a damn stinking thing myself. That fellow was a SeeBee in the Pacific for three years, and it's not right—"

"Right or wrong's not the point. The point is that people don't like that sort of talk from black boys down here. You'll lose us business. Business is slack enough in summer as it is. Listen, my boy, let me tell you one thing right how. If you've come up here for more money, it's no soap. I haven't any cause keeping that program on the air the way things are going. I'm really not justified."

"Mr. Logan, in a way I'm relieved to hear you say that. What I came up here to tell you is that I'm quitting at the end of the week."

"Why, you—" His chair tilted forward with a loud bang, and he slapped the palms of both hands hard on the desk. "Why, you son of a bitch!" He said it in a tone of pleasant surprise, more entertained at his own astonishment than angered at me. "What's up, anyway?"

"I've had an offer—more of a gamble than anything else—but I want to try it. It's a new kind of show that I think has possibilities."

"What kind of show?"

"You can tune in on it next Sunday at nine if you're interested. It's going to originate here in Washington at the home of a Mrs. Finchley."

"Martha Finchley?"

"Do you know her?"

"I'll say I know her. She's a nut."

I recalled Martha's remark about him. Apparently their dislike was mutual and ardent. "Better watch out for That One," he was saying. "Better keep your eyes open around that dame; better wear a bulletproof vest when you do business with her; better—" He went on and on, advising me of more and more picturesque precautions.

I ventured to interrupt. "What did she ever do to you?"

"Do to me!" he screamed. "I'll tell you what she did to me! I was her husband's best friend. When they moved over to S Street she never once asked me to step inside that house, not even for a minute, not even for a drink of water. Why? Because I'm not good enough. I'm just a diamond merchant, just a dirty businessman, same as her husband was. What she wants around her are big shots, pansies in striped pants, greaseballs with accents." He threw back his head and brayed with laughter. "Boy, you better watch out for That One."

I hoped he'd go on. I wanted to hear more about my Mrs. Finchley, who was turning out to have as many facets as a Logan diamond. Or was it rather that she had only one which she flashed variously in various directions? "We daughters of the finest state in the union must get together." "She never asked me inside her house—what she wants are big shots." And in that soft, cooing voice of Mr. San Martin: "She is delighted. Nothing pleases her more than the storming of the fort."

"By the way"—Mr. Logan squinted out of his pouchy round eyes at me—"how'd you happen to connect with That One?"

I skipped the Incident in the French-camp version of our meeting and explained how she'd heard my broadcasts and decided to call me.

"Uh-huh." Mr. Logan nodded his head in a half-dozen decisive little jerks. "Sounds like her method. That One doesn't know the word 'ethical.' Steps right in and buys you off under my nose."

"But, Mr. Logan—" I began.

The buzzer on his desk rang and he picked up the phone.

"No," he said, "I've changed my mind. Something urgent came up. Absolutely no." He slapped the phone down on its cradle.

"My wife wants me to go to a garden party," he grunted. "I should stand around and get mosquito bites on my ankles and caterpillars in my drink. Which reminds me, my boy, of a very special garden party that used to take place on S Street every summer. Oscar Finchley put his foot down. Once a year, he told that wife of his, once a year she had to invite all his old friends. So she invited us every July out into her back yard. Oh, it was quite a party," he admitted grudgingly, "buffet table a mile long, two dozen waiters, string quartet under the trees, champagne fountain—"

"What was that?"

"She had a regular contraption rigged up with four spouts and champagne pouring from each one. Who else would think of such a thing? And she'd be gliding around in a garden-party dress from Mainbocher, putting on the charm act. . . . I tell you, Oscar was a beaten man."

"He died before the war, didn't he?"

"Sure he died. Who could have lived long with her? He'd come home, the drawing room would be filled with these diplomats talking gibberish he couldn't understand. He'd go into his library, there would be some bureaucrats using his phone. He'd go down in his bar, there would be a bunch of politicians guzzling his liquor and giving him dirty looks. They didn't know he owned the joint. He used to cry on my shoulder about it. 'You know what I married?' he'd say. 'A woman who's trying to be President of the United States.'" Mr. Logan stopped suddenly and drew a couple of long puffs on his cigar. "What's she doing promoting a radio show?" he asked.

I shrugged.

"Who's paying the bill?"

"The Finchley Stores are sponsoring it."

"Sure, that means she's the sponsor. So what's she sponsoring? A radio program? Entertainment for the old folks at home? Like hell she is. You don't have to tell me what the show is all about, but I'll tell you something. The minute I hear it, if and when it goes on, I'll be able to tell you what she's got on her mind, what it's all about. That is," he added, "unless I'm a lot dumber than I used to be."

After a while we talked of other things and made a lunch date to discuss a possible successor for me on the Logan program and I said good-by. When I reached the door Mr. Logan called to me. He was leaning way back in his chair with his feet up on the desk and cigar smoke in curling white clouds above him.

"Did you ever hear of a steel jock strap, my boy?" he shouted. "You're going to need one!"

9

When I got home Saturday in the late afternoon Frances Rhodes was on duty at the switchboard.

"Hello," I said, "where've you been all week?"

"On mah vacation," she said, pronouncing it like a true daughter of Georgia, which she was.

"Where'd you go?"

"Nowheah. Spent most of mah time lookin' for a job. Another job, that is."

So she'd gotten tired of our building manager, I thought. This middle-aged glamour boy was, because of his power over suite rentals, one of the crown princes of Washington that summer. There was literally nothing he couldn't get in exchange for a cubbyhole in the Webster Apartments. I suspected that he didn't provide Frances with an apartment in exchange for switchboard services only.

"Are you leaving us, Frances?"

She shook her head. "No luck this time. Ah guess Ah haven't any qualifications."

"What news from the lieutenant?"

"Nothin' new. He's still sittin' in Manila. Ah don't know when he'll evah get home. Ah think the Army's plumb forgot about him. Ah think maybe they've lost his papahs and don't know he's alive."

Her fuzzy-edged brown eyes filled with tears which might have spilled over if the board hadn't buzzed just then. I waited while she plugged in the call. She was not much over twenty years old, a pretty, plump girl, always dressed in frills and ruffles. She should have been wearing flowers in her long thick hair instead of earphones. She should have been dancing with that lieutenant of hers or strolling under the magnolia trees or whatever they do down there in Macon. "Danny thinks Ah'm a miracle woman to have an apartment waitin' on him," she'd said to me once. "He thinks Ah'm jist wonderful!" She had laughed, showing all her little white teeth, but there had been no echo of mirth in her eyes.

Now she slipped the earphones down around her neck and handed me two slips of paper. One was a message to call Miss Hoyt at a Hobart number. The other was from Geraldine Hudock, asking me to pick her up at an address off Columbia Road instead of meeting her at the Shoreham.

"You steppin' out tonight, Mr. Pike?" Frances asked.

"In a manner of speaking."

She tossed her head, and her hair rippled along her shoulders. "That's right nice," she said. "Ah think it's good for folks to enjoy themselves."

Here's the way I figured out Geraldine's change of mind. If the girls knew something peculiar about Benson's death which they were afraid of revealing, Geraldine would not even have talked to me that day in the Navy Building, nor gone to lunch, nor made another date. And if they were terrified by my prying into the thing, Geraldine would not have called and left her address today. She had relaxed, as Mr. San Martin would put it—and so the whole affair was adding up to nothing. This later proved to be an upside-down way of thinking, but for the moment it fooled me.

After my shower I turned the electric fan directly on the chair near the telephone, sat down in it naked, lighted a cigarette, and dialed Hobart 8873. The ubiquitous Southern voice answered, a maid who said she would call Miss Hoyt. Through the earpiece I could hear the sound of laughter and loud talk, a dog barking, and then the tinkle of a glass close to the phone and the bang it made as someone put it down hard.

"Hello, hello?" said Enid, her voice very high, very gay.

"Hello. This is—"

"I know, I know. Listen here, Alexander Pike, we're having a wonderful party. Hear it?" She rattled her glass close to the phone. "Put on some clothes and scoot right down here."

In spite of myself I blinked at the phone. "Now I understand how you get those juicy items for your column," I told her. "You have a one-way television set."

"Don't I wish it!" She giggled. "When you've been in Washington for as many summers as I have you know the first thing anybody does at home is strip. Now come on," she coaxed, "put on that little ole seersucker suit and scoot over. I want you to meet some friends of mine, some very civilized people—"

"I'm sorry, Enid, I can't make it. I have an engagement and—"

"But you must," she wailed. "There isn't a man over five feet ten in the house except Chet Langley, and he doesn't count because he's going to be horizontal in ten minutes."

"So that's my hold over you! And all the time I thought it was my irresistible corn-fed Ohio charm—"

"Look, Alec, if you scoot over here now I'll tell you all about how it feels to be a female, six feet one and five eighths inches tall. It's a whole way of life, believe me. Look, Alec, could I bribe you with a very juicy tidbit from tomorrow's column? Now scoot over and I'll whisper it in your ear."

"That wouldn't be cricket, would it?"

"I'd do it for you. You're so civilized. Look, why don't you bring your engagement over here?"

"It's not that kind—it's business."

Her high laugh tinkled through the earpiece. "If that's what you want to call it," she said. "Now you and Martha be careful and don't overwork yourselves."

Before I could explain her mistake she rang off.

Afterward I had a queer guilty feeling, as if I'd let Enid down in some way. But hell, I hardly knew her. I didn't know her at all. Some of the things she had said at Martha's house the other night began to make sense, and the eager warmth with which she had greeted me. Maybe that long-boned stretched-out body of hers explained her column too. Maybe she compensated for it by being cute and coy in print. When I read her Saturday offering a few minutes later it no longer seemed so silly. It was like looking at one of those puzzle drawings they used to print in children's magazines: right side up the picture is a maze of nonsensical patterns and lines, but turn it upside down and it becomes the face of a woman.

There was an item in the column about Carlos San Martin.

> *Carlos San Martin, handsome and dashing Georgetown antique and art dealer (he demonstrated the art of the samba at Martha Finchley's the other night), is in New York this week end powwowing with refugee nobility over some knickknacks brought out of their lost palaces. You can pick up same at his shop soon, but be*

sure those pockets are well lined. These trifles
will be but expensive!

At a quarter to seven I drove along Gorden Street
N.W., looking for Geraldine's number. The houses were
mostly red brick three-story buildings with English base-
ments and stone-front steps. Here and there in a front bay
window hung a bird cage (that badge of loneliness), or a
pot of dusty ivy, or a rare "Rooms" sign. The glass curtains seemed all to have been cut from one unappetizing
bolt of tan mesh. These places had known better days, but
now, shabby and run down, they housed hordes of un-
attached Washingtonians known as "roomers"—a class of
human beings not affluent enough to be called "tenants,"
nor cherished enough to be called "guests."

Geraldine's house looked, if possible, a bit more for-
lorn than the others. It had been rubbish-collection day,
and a few battered ash cans still stood on its curb. In the
front hall, which smelled of worn carpeting and the inevitable fried food, a young man with a discharge button in
his lapel stood reading his mail. I asked him where to find
Miss Hudock and, hardly looking up from his letter, he
directed me to the third floor, door on the right.

I climbed up, and just as I reached the third-floor
landing a door opened and Gloria Hart stood poised on
the threshold. The first thing I noticed was that she was
beautiful. The other night, worn out by two hours in a
tear-jerking movie, she had merely been very pretty. She
wore a long filmy black dress with no shoulder straps and
a big red flower at the waist.

"Hello, Mr. Pike," she said.

"How are you, Miss Hart?"

"Come in, won't you?"

I stepped into the kind of room one sees sometimes in
linoleum ads, but this one had no linoleum. It did have,

however, a tricky do-it-over-yourself look; old furniture painted white, and pictures suspended from velvet bow-knots, that sort of thing. I sat down on a studio couch covered with a flounce of cretonne, and Gloria handed me a cigarette.

"Don't you have to be hurrying off somewhere or other?" I asked her.

"Why, no. Why?"

"After the other night I—"

"Oh," she said. "That was awfully silly, wasn't it? The only way I can explain it, Mr. Pike, is that—well, suddenly I realized I hadn't done a very ladylike thing—letting a stranger pick me up—and, well—you know, that was one rule my mother always insisted upon back home."

"Did your mother ever tell you a girl can break her neck jumping out of an automobile?"

Her cheeks dimpled with incongruous naivete. "I guess she figured that if I obeyed her I'd never have to."

"Suppose you tell me how it happened that when I mentioned the name Harvey Benson the other night you immediately thought of dear old Mom?"

This time she projected a ringing little laugh that sounded as if it had been written right into the stage directions. "You aren't going to stay angry at me for that foolishness, are you, Mr. Pike? I apologize. I really do."

It was apparent that the cross-examination method wasn't going to get me very far. Some time and some thought would have to be spent on a method of extracting information from this baby.

"Where's Geraldine?" I asked her.

"Oh, I should have told you right away, Mr. Pike. Geraldine called and said she was terribly sorry, her boss asked her to work tonight. Something important came up."

"When did she find that out?"

"Just a little while ago. She just telephoned. She felt just awful."

"I suppose the Navy comes first. Have you a telephone? I'll call the Shoreham and cancel my reservation."

"There's a phone in the hall, but—"

"But?"

"Well, I'm not doing anything this evening and I thought—"

"You thought?"

"Maybe you'd let me substitute for Geraldine."

She dropped both her voice and her eyes—another stage direction straight out of the senior-class play.

"An excellent idea," I agreed, as if I'd read the script. "Especially since by some lucky coincidence you're dressed up and ready to go."

"That's awfully sweet of you, Mr. Pike." She gave me what I took to be a most inviting stare. She was small and, with her round face and fluffy yellow hair, the type of girl referred to in my father's day as a "doll." As she walked across the room to get her wrap from the closet I noticed, however, that she handled her compact little body without any of the innocence that word implies. And that black dress wasn't innocent, either, with its non-visible supports and her smooth bare shoulders white above it. I began to feel slightly expectant about the evening. It had been a long time since I'd gone out with a girl like Gloria. I hadn't realized how much I'd been missing it.

When we came down the steps the same young man was still standing in the hall. This time his letter proved less absorbing. He looked up and remained looking.

"Hello, Jack," Gloria said as we passed him.

I saw his gaze shift to me, and suddenly he laughed out loud, a smug laugh full of suppressed delight.

"Who's he?" I asked.

"Oh, just a boy—lives in the house."

"What struck him so funny?"

"Oh, he's just a psychoneurotic," she answered airily. "He thinks everything's funny."

No one laughed when we walked through the huge, handsome lobby of the Shoreham, but plenty of heads turned as Gloria went by, her pert nose haughtily in the air, her gait sheer exhibitionism. It was in the lobby, too, that I first really noticed her wrap. It was a short cape of white fur—not bunny fur. This little singer-turned-secretary was wearing summer ermine, at least a thousand dollars' worth of it.

Our table was a good one in the center section of the room, and Gloria seemed pleased. She looked around at the crowd thickly sprinkled with high-echelon uniforms and well-dressed bejeweled ladies.

"Quite a change from last night," she said.

"Where were you last night?"

"Out with Jack. That boy back at the house. He took me to a Hot Shoppe. Hamburgers and talk, talk, talk."

"You don't like conversation?"

"Of course I do. *Interesting* conversation."

The waiter appeared at that moment, and we ordered martinis and the soft-shell crabs. When he had gone I said, "To get back to conversation, I'd like to have some with you on a certain subject. Whether it will be interesting or not depends upon you."

"I'll do my best." The dimple twinkled in and out.

"I want to know how Harvey Benson died."

She looked at me with candid eyes. She even picked up a glass and took a drink of water, as if to show me how steady her hand was, how unruffled my request left her.

"Why, I told you already," she reproached me mildly. "He committed suicide. He drowned himself."

The girl was good. I promoted her out of the senior-class play into one of those ingenue parts in a Hollywood murder mystery. I told her so.

"I don't know what you mean," she said.

"I mean you're such a sweet little actress. It's a shame for you to be wasting your talent behind some guy's typewriter. Now snap out of that innocent-bystander role and tell me what I want to know. Because I'm going to find out, whether you tell me or not."

She gave me a round-eyed baby stare. "You don't have to threaten me, Mr. Pike. I'll be glad to tell you everything I know, but first don't you think you ought to explain why you're playing the D.A. with me? What's the idea?"

"Harvey Benson was a friend of mine."

"So he was a friend of yours. Maybe I'm not sentimental enough, but I don't see why his being a friend of yours makes you do things like dating Geraldine."

"What's wrong with that? She's a nice girl."

"But the only reason you're interested in her is because she lives with me and because you think I know something about Benson."

"Maybe. If I'd known it was so simple to date you on a Saturday evening I might have tried to go about it in a less complicated way. But Geraldine's still a nice girl."

She drained her cocktail glass and put it down on the table, twirling the stem between her fingers. "Tit for tat. You tell me why you're so interested in Benson and I'll tell you what I know."

"He was my friend."

"You're repeating yourself, Mr. Pike."

"All right," I said, "I can't tell you because I don't know the answer to that one myself. Benson and I weren't even what you'd call buddies; we didn't see each other often enough for that. But when we were together we were good friends immediately. I've seen a lot of friends come and go in the past few years and I have a hell of a lot on my mind now without sticking my nose into Benson's business. Anyway, if I do find out everything wasn't hunky-dory about the way he died, what good will it do him? You see, the moral of this long speech is that there isn't a reason in the world why I should be interested in Benson." She stopped twirling the glass. "But before you go on taking a deep breath of relief, angel-puss, let me tell you this. I don't happen to need anything so goddamned logical as a reason for anything I do."

"Uh-huh," she said, "it was just idle curiosity."

I lifted an eyebrow at that. If I know you, baby, I thought, you don't have an idle idea in your bean.

The waiter arrived with his tray of silver-covered dishes, and while we were waiting for him to serve us I took a good look around. There was the usual sprinkling of celebrities in the Sapphire Room that night. That was one thing I liked about Washington. When you saw a man who looked like Attorney General Tom Clark it was Attorney General Tom Clark. That night, too, the woman at a nearby table who looked like Gloria Swanson was Gloria Swanson. Four Navy captains in handsome and immaculate white were with her. I pointed her out to Gloria.

Perhaps if Miss Swanson hadn't been there the lieutenant passing by wouldn't have been so eager to stop and greet his superiors, and in that large room I might have missed seeing him altogether. (In which case things would have developed differently for a while.) Gloria saw him, too, but from her lack of reaction it was apparent she didn't know him. After his introduction to the actress was over and the compliment of his awed and admiring stare paid, the lieutenant joined a man and a girl already seated at a small table, luckily not too far from ours. I could keep an eye on him.

The waiter went away, leaving on our plates three tiny browned crabs scuttled beside their burial mounds of cole-slaw.

"Now about Benson," I reminded Gloria.

"All right, Mr. Pike." She picked up her knife and fork and slashed at the crabs with almost too much concentration. "This is all I know. It happened while our unit was hanging around Rome waiting for transportation to France. There was going to be a few days' delay, and Harvey wanted to drive up to the mountains. He'd been invited to visit by some big-shot Italian who had a villa on Fucino. He asked me to come along for company. He'd been having trouble with his wife, you know."

"I didn't know."

"She was the patriotic type. Waited till he got overseas and then wrote him she wanted a divorce. He was awfully depressed about it. I tried my best to cheer him up."

"How?"

"I told him she couldn't be worth a damn if she'd do such a thing. I told him there were plenty of other girls in the world—"

"And fish in the sea, and stars in the sky, and eggs in the basket. I heard various versions of that speech when my wife and I split up. People deliver it with the best of intentions, but it doesn't help."

"Of course not," she said eagerly. "It doesn't help a bit. That's why Harvey drowned himself."

"Maybe. In novels people sometimes kill themselves when a girl walks out, but not me. Not Harvey. But go on."

"Harvey borrowed a jeep, and we drove up to this place on Fucino. I never paid much attention to off-stage scenery before, but, gee, this place was gorgeous. Awfully romantic, with a full moon and the lake like glass. I could tell that all these romantic-looking surroundings were making

Harvey feel lower and lower, so when this Italian suggested we take a sail on the lake I was relieved. I thought it
would take his mind off himself."

"Didn't you think going out on the lake might be dangerous in his state of mind?"

Again she got very busy with her knife and fork. "You
never dream a person you know is going to do a thing like
that. Anyway, all I can tell you about the rest of it is what
this Italian told me."

"Weren't you on the boat?"

"No. I didn't go. I get seasick."

"Even when the lake's like glass?"

She put her fork down and wiped her mouth with the
napkin. I remember with what dismay she stared at the
little red streak her lipstick left on the linen, as if she had
committed a grave social error. "Well," she said at last,
"it was getting a bit choppy by then, by the time he made
the suggestion. Anyway, they went out, and when Harvey
jumped off the boat it was hard for this Italian to turn
around and search for him because it was so choppy, see?
They found his body in the morning."

"Wasn't there an investigation?"

"Oh, sure. The Army investigated and announced it
was a suicide. Naturally." She gazed at her decapitated
crabs. "Poor Harvey."

"By the way, what was the name of your Italian host?"

"Oh, one of those Eytie names. They all sound alike. I
can't remember."

"Do you suppose you could try very hard and remember it for me?"

She picked a cigarette butt out of the ash tray and
ground it down. The pressure burst the paper, and the
loose tobacco poured out.

"Gee, I'm dumb," she said. "I just can't remember."

Suddenly the movement of the Navy lieutenant caught my eye. He was escorting the girl from his table to the dance floor. I sprang to my feet too. "Come on," I commanded Gloria, "this is where we dance."

On the crowded floor I lost the lieutenant. I remembered vaguely that his partner's dress was a flowered pattern, but the floor seemed to be filled with Navy officers and girls in print dresses. I circled about as hastily as I could, pulling Gloria with me, her bewildered face pressed to my chest.

"Sorry," I apologized. "I'm out of practice "

"What's the rush?" she panted.

I saw an opening and edged in toward the center of the floor. Gloria tripped after me, and I felt the toe of her slipper under my foot.

"Ouch," she said loudly and a little hysterically, and a voice behind me said, "What are you doing to that poor girl, Pike?"

With joy I spun around. "Hello, you old slave driver," I greeted the lieutenant. The curly-haired brunette on his arm regarded Gloria sympathetically.

"What do you mean by that crack?" he asked.

"What do you mean keeping little Miss Hudock working overtime while you're out disporting yourself?"

"You're crazy. Hudock left like a bat out of hell at noon. What's it to you, anyway?"

I had felt Gloria stiffen as he spoke. "By the way," I said to her, "I want you to meet Geraldine's boss. Miss Hart, Lieutenant Shaver."

He introduced us to his girl, and after a few more admonishments about my dancing they vanished into the crowd. Gloria looked up at me, her eyebrows raised and the tip of her tongue showing between her lips like a kid caught stealing jam.

"Why did you lie to me?"

"Because I like you. I liked you right away. I was jealous of Geraldine when she told me you made a date with her."

"What did you tell her about tonight?"

"I told her you telephoned and called off the date because you had to go out of town. So she went to an early movie with one of her girl friends."

"And why did you do all this again?"

"Because I like you so much."

About an hour later we were sitting on Mr. Pearse's overstuffed green brocade davenport. Suddenly Gloria leaped up and walked across the room.

"For a girl who says she likes me so much," I complained, "you seem to find me awfully repulsive."

"Oh no." The dim bulb in the table lamp made a high light on her sullen lipsticked mouth, right now a little messy at the edges. "I just wanted to get a cigarette."

"I have cigarettes over here."

"Have you? This is a very nice apartment."

"Would you like to see the rest of it? There's a bedroom with a wonderful southwest exposure."

"No, thank you, I'm—I'm a bit tired."

"Then come on over here beside me and rest awhile."

She walked toward me as if a heavy spring were holding her to the opposite wall. I pulled her down on the davenport. "Now, that's better," I said. "Now tell me exactly what it is about me that you like so much." Her hair was soft and perfumed and her ear was soft and nervous as a squirrel's. "You know you went to a lot of trouble to come out with me tonight, didn't you? Didn't you?"

Beneath my mouth her mouth moaned a yes. Beneath my hand her shoulder quivered. She pulled away and got to her feet.

"I—I think I'd like a drink of water," she said desperately.

"All right. Come on into the kitchen."

After I had turned on the water to let it run cold, I cornered her in front of the cupboard. She leaned away from me until she was almost doing a back bend into the bread-box.

"Sure you won't have something stronger?" I asked her. "Positive? Certain?" She was wagging her head back and forth. Her eyes were as hard and as blue as a couple of agates. "By the way, you haven't recalled that Italian's name yet, have you?"

"No." Her lips twitched in a wan attempt at a smile. "I wish I could, but I just can't."

"You know," I said, "I'm glad you like me so much. I could go for you in a small way."

"Oh-oh," she tittered. "Just in a small way, Mr. Pike?"

"Alec. In a big way, then. Do you like that better? Hmmm?" I kissed her shoulder. "Washington's been the loneliest town for me until now," I murmured. "You and I are going to have a lot of fun together, angel-puss."

"Yes," she gasped.

"Why shouldn't we start now?"

"No," she gasped.

"Is there someone else?"

"Well, no. Well, yes."

"Is he rich and handsome?"

"Well . . ."

"Did he buy you that pretty little ermine jacket? This lovely dress?" I ran my hands down her slender sides over the filmy black material. "Did he buy this lovely dress right out of Erlebacher's window? I don't stand a chance with a guy like that around, do I?"

"Yes, you do," she said wearily.

I put my hands on her shoulders and held her away from me. "You don't say that as if you mean it," I reproached her. "Do you know what I've been thinking? I've been thinking that you don't really like me at all. That you just say you do. You lied to Geraldine and me tonight and you came out with me because you want to find out something. Like for example how much I know about what happened to Harvey Benson and what I intend to do about it. Isn't that true?" She didn't answer. I shook her roughly. "Isn't that true?"

"Why, no," she said, her eyes filling with tears, "no, it isn't."

"Who put you up to this? Who asked you to find out about me?"

"Nobody."

"Then what did you come for?"

"Because—because I like you." Her voice was weak, but she was sticking to her lines. Whoever planned out this dialogue for her had coached her well.

"In that case, angel-puss," I said, "there's a word for you. You know what you are, don't you? You're a goddamn tease." I pushed her away and she stumbled against the cupboard. Then I went into the other room to get her jacket.

On the way to her house we didn't speak. But when I drew up to the curb in front of the ash cans I said, "Still can't remember the name of that Italian gent that you and Harvey visited?"

She turned to me with a flashing dimpled smile, for by that time she had recovered entirely from our little scene.

"Oh no," she said vehemently, "not in a thousand years."

She leaped out of the car and ran up the steps. Watching her, I thought of the young man in the hall who had laughed so loudly as we went out. I understood now why he'd done it.

10

The telephone woke me at ten o'clock Sunday morning. I stumbled out of bed and into the living room to answer.

"Hello, Mr. Pike," said a scared-sounding thin voice. "I—I hope I didn't wake you. This is Geraldine Hudock."

"Why, hello," I said. "I was very sorry about last night. I didn't know they ever worked you so late down there on a Saturday. Planning another war or something?"

"So Gloria told you I was working," she said bitterly. "She lied to you. I wasn't working at all. She lied to me too. She told me you telephoned and canceled our date. But she forgot one little thing, such as that I might see you bring her home. I was opening the window last night and I saw your car drive up."

"Why do you suppose she did that?"

"I don't know. She doesn't care what she does, just so she gets what she's after. I hate her."

"What is it that your cousin is after, Geraldine?"

"Men, I guess. She's man-crazy. She can't stand seeing a man pay attention to anyone else besides herself. That's part of the reason why I didn't want you to call for me at home. But I didn't suspect she'd think up a dirty trick like that when I told her I was meeting you at the Shoreham."

"Did you say anything to her when she got upstairs last night?"

"No. I felt so bad I pretended to be asleep. I didn't want her to see me crying."

"Listen, Geraldine," I said, "if you're not busy tonight, how about going to a party with me? It's one those big open-house things—I think you'd like it."

"Thanks a lot, Mr. Pike, but you don't have to make it up to me. That's not why I called. I called to tell you something you might be interested in—something about that man you mentioned the other night, that Mr. Benson. Gloria was on the boat with him when he drowned."

"How do you know that?" I demanded.

"She told me once. She made me promise never to breathe it to anyone, but after what she's done to me I don't keep promises for her."

"Just what did she tell you?"

"That's all. She wouldn't say another word about what happened. She acted awfully mysterious and important and as if she was mixed up in something way over my head. She just told me to impress me. You see, the other night when you suddenly mentioned him out of a clear sky—that's why she got so excited and made me get out of the car with her."

"Did she say anything more about it after you left me?"

"No. She just said she didn't want to be asked any questions about that Mr. Benson by anybody. She said that whatever happened was all over a long time ago and she didn't want to get mixed up in it any more. Like fun she didn't. Then why'd she break her neck to go out with you?"

"Who does your cousin work for, Miss Hudock?"

"I don't even know. She doesn't tell me. That's another one of her mysteries. But there's something funny about it, I'll guarantee that. She says she's a secretary. Why, she, can't even type! She sang in a New York night club before she went overseas, and then when she got back she moved down here with me and suddenly she's a secretary."

"Then you haven't any idea where she works?"

"I wish I knew. I'd like to get a job there myself. What-ever she makes must be plenty, the way she buys clothes. I'm sorry I can't tell you more, but you seemed curious about that Mr. Benson, and I just thought I'd tell you about Gloria. I don't consider any promise sacred after what she did. Would you?"

"No indeed, Geraldine, I wouldn't either. Now how about tonight? The party, incidentally, is at Mrs. Martha Finchley's."

"Oh yes, I know." Her voice was reverent. "You're going to do the broadcast. I've been reading about it in the papers. I was going to listen to it tonight."

"Then come with me and watch it as well."

"Oh—I—I'd love to."

"At seven-thirty then."

"I'll be ready, Mr. Pike."

She rang off and I went back to bed—but not to sleep. So Gloria hadn't been hanging around inside somebody's villa when Harvey went out on the lake. So Gloria had been on the boat with him when he was drowned. This only strengthened what I had supposed already from last night. Gloria knew what happened on that boat—and she wasn't telling. Gloria was the key. I thought of her petu-lant and pretty face above the ermine jacket. *Whatever she makes, it must be plenty, the way she buys clothes.* I could play at being a gumshoe and follow her, I thought, watch her tomorrow morning and see where she does go to work.

When I called for Geraldine she was dressed in a light blue dress with a fluff around the neck and a pink-pink flower in the belt. She looked like a lost bridesmaid from a very sad wedding. There was no sign of Gloria.

"Where's the little storyteller?" I asked.

"She's out." Geraldine's tone was still aggrieved. "She said she had a date with a man from her office."

"What building is her office in, do you know?"

She shook her head.

"Maybe she doesn't work at all."

"Then where would she get all that money?"

"Maybe someone is paying her just for being her own sweet self."

"You mean—" Her bony face flushed. "Oh no, I'm sure she has a job of some kind. She has ink on her hands sometimes and she told me she learned to run a switchboard."

"What time does she leave in the morning?"

"She says she leaves a half-hour after I do, and I leave at seven-thirty."

That meant I ought to be on the job a few minutes before eight if there was to be any research done on the little blonde's habits.

Cars were parked for blocks up and down S Street and around all the corners, and a line of limousines moved slowly along as each stopped to allow the occupants to alight in front of the door. I finally found a small place up the street between a fire hydrant and a driveway into which the Crosley fitted perfectly. I helped Geraldine out and we joined a stream of people walking toward the house. Every window was blazing with light. Between the curtains on the second floor we could see that a large and festive crowd was already on hand.

The butler opened the door and directed us to the coat rooms. I came out first and stood in the entrance hall beside a statue of a little Nubian slave with a card tray on his head and listened to the commotion upstairs. Through the loud talk and the twitter of laughter came the strains of an accordion playing "Star Dust." In a few minutes Geraldine appeared, her mouth relipsticked and her face pale.

As we went upstairs I noticed some of the other women giving her the Washington Eye. This is a look made up equally of graciousness and disdain—a mixture damned difficult to achieve but necessary in Washington, where most people bow to necessity. The graciousness was for you if you were somebody or married to a somebody. The disdain was just in case you were nobody and so that you'd not think you were being given a friendly signal into the rarefied atmosphere above you. For the people able to cast about an eye like that, everything was solved. Geraldine was dressed with exactly the right amount of dowdiness to scare the pants off the other females. Only a girl who was securely and permanently in the top ranks would dare to appear at Martha Finchley's looking like a lost bridesmaid.

The drawing room, the wide hall, and the dining room were packed with people. Several waiters carrying trays covered with mosaics of hors d'oeuvres and martinis inched their way through the crush. A curly-haired young man in a tuxedo was playing the accordion; for money, obviously, not for love. As I watched, a general, aglitter with stars on expertly cut gabardine, tapped him on the shoulder. A moment later his instrument bellowed the Army Air Corps song, but the young man's expression of slumbrous detachment did not change. Over the rooms like a cloud hung the smell of a hundred brands of perfume, of gin and cigarette smoke, of anchovies and olives. The whole scene seemed feverish, like something on a double-fast movie film, the gestures too jerky, the voices too high-pitched, and, judging from the laughter, the jokes too funny. And then there were the Eyes again. Everybody seemed to be facing the archway over the top of the stairs where newcomers were first to be seen. If one of these watchers got turned around or if his line of vision was intercepted in some way he restlessly maneuvered for position until his eyes were in the right direction once more.

When their bright and curious combined glare was turned on us, Geraldine's hand tightened in mine. I felt perspiration stippling my lip and temples. A tray of cocktails went by and I snatched two.

"Take a long drink," I said to Geraldine. "It will help you through the line-up."

Then I saw Martha pushing her way toward us. She was wrapped like a mummy in a sheath of gray satin that high-lighted every convexity of her body. As always, her face was plaster-white and cool, and there was a sparkle of diamonds at her throat and ears.

"Alec! Alec!" she called. "Thank God you're here. I've got stage fright. The men are in the library now, setting up the microphone. I took one look at it and got the shakes."

"Hello, Martha," I said, "I'd like to introduce—"

"A man from *Variety* called," Martha interrupted. "For once in my life I didn't know what to tell a reporter. Would you take a look in the library and check—"

"Sure. Right away, But I'd like you to meet—"

"Lloyd is being so wonderfully calm about it. You'd think he was used to talking into a million homes every night in the—"

"There won't be quite a million," I said. "This is Miss—"

"Alec, I'm going to round up our special guests so you can meet them first and instruct them—"

"Martha, listen," I said desperately, "I've brought a friend. I want you to meet Miss Hudock."

Martha's mouth stayed open, but no sound came from it. For the first time she noticed the girl, at my side. Her glance skimmed the lank hair, the glasses, the blue dress, and what she saw allowed her to be generous. She gave Geraldine her most dazzling smile and took both of the girl's limp hands in her own.

"I'm so glad to meet you, Miss Hudock," she said.

"How do you do, Mrs. Finchley," Geraldine said.

"Well, it certainly is a pleasure to have you here. Are you visiting in Washington?"

"No. I work here in the Navy Department. You don't remember, probably, but we've met once before—"

Just then a little white-haired man with a black mustache and big black eyes rushed up and lifted Martha's fingers to his lips.

"My darling," he murmured, "the gown is perfect. I am overjoyed to see you."

So this was Mr. San Martin. Under the bright lights he looked as he had sounded, like a very, very slick article. His hair was prematurely white, and beneath it his face was smooth and impudent.

"Ah, Mr. Pike," he said, "we meet without the cloak of darkness." He stared at me with sly, smiling eyes. "And how are the suicide investigations coming along?"

"Very well," I said. "Why?"

"Oh, I am interested in the subject—purely as a moral question. Does one have the right to drown himself? It is an enticing ethical problem, you know."

I wanted to ask him how he had happened to guess that Benson had drowned himself. I was positive I hadn't mentioned it that night on the terrace.

But Martha was saying, "Carlos, I want you to meet Mr. Pike's friend, Miss Hudock, I understand she practically runs the Navy Building."

Mr. San Martin kissed Geraldine's trembling fingers.

"Will you and Miss Hudock get something to eat and then see what's going on in the library?" Martha asked again. "I'm going to get Lloyd and the others, and we'll meet you there in a few minutes."

She turned away and was engulfed in the crowd.

It took me about ten minutes to negotiate Geraldine over to the literally groaning board of the buffet. We could take our choice of turkey, baked ham, roast beef, or lobster Newburg, and everything that went with them. There was also a large bucket carved from solid ice and filled to the brim with caviar. We ran into Mrs. Seabright in front of it. She had a highball in one hand and a spaniel-faced man with sideburns in the other.

"So you don't understand where his money comes from?" she was demanding. "He's one of the biggest lobbyists down here. There's no end to the funds those people will provide once they think they've got a champion. I told Lloyd we've got to match what they spend by spending ten times more." Then she saw us and her face broke into one of those tight automatic smiles she bestowed on everyone.

"Why, hello, Mr. Pike," she said, "this is Mr. Harrington."

I told them Geraldine's name. The spaniel-faced man bowed and said good evening and that he was charmed with the introduction or some such thing.

"Oh yes," said Mrs. Seabright, folding her lips back again, "someone just pointed you out to me. Now which of the admirals is your father again?"

The show went on at nine o'clock as scheduled. When it was over everyone said it had been excellent listening. It is difficult to describe a radio show, especially one so fluid and spontaneous. I can only say that to me every second of it was entertaining and informative. I think we did what the opening announcement said we'd do—allowed our listening audience to be "among those present" at Martha Finchley's house on S Street. I had to agree with everyone else, that Lloyd Seabright had put on a brilliant performance. In fact, he shone so brightly during the discussions that our three guests, a Cabinet member noted for his wit, an attaché from a hot news embassy, and a prominent columnist, had appeared dim stars by comparison. I know that I had that good, glowing, satisfied feeling inside that I always get when things have clicked exactly right.

The party was over by twelve. Downstairs in the wide circle of the hall, where the indirect lighting was effective on her face and gown, Martha stood saying good night, and it was wonderful of you to come, and thank you, I think it went off very well too, and several times I heard her say yes, he was perfectly splendid, wasn't he, because someone had mentioned Lloyd.

The Seabrights and Geraldine and I were the last to come down.

"Oh, you're not going too!" Martha cried when she saw us. "I thought we'd have another drink and some postmortems."

"But, my dear, everyone says the show is a hit. It's all settled," said Mrs. Seabright. She swung her arm in a broad and dizzy circle. "Hurray for our side," she declaimed like a pupil in an elocution school, and for the first time I realized she was drunk.

"The point is," Martha said coldly, "can we trust the opinions of everyone who was here?"

"The outside reactions, the ones we'll get tomorrow, are what count," Lloyd said. "I told you the governor phoned—"

"Oh, Alec"—Martha turned to me—"I didn't have a chance to tell you. The governor was very pleased. 'Immensely gratified' is how he put it, and he has reason to be our severest critic. Don't you think his reaction is a good sign?"

I nodded, and Mrs. Seabright grasped my sleeve. She was wearing a jeweled band in her hair, but even this Alice-in-Wonderland effect combined with the artful lighting did not improve her gaunt face or its wide, demented smile. "Can we drop you and Miss Hudock anywhere?" she asked. "Our car is outside."

"No, thanks, I have mine up the street," I told her.

I shook hands with Martha. "Thanks and good night," I said. "It was quite an evening." What I really wanted to say to her I couldn't say there in front of the others. "I'll phone you tomorrow," I said.

I told Geraldine to wait inside until I brought the car down.

"Just a minute," Lloyd said, "I'll walk with you. I'm parked up the street too."

"Did you drive yourself?" Martha asked. "Where's Henry tonight?"

"I gave him the week end off—" The door closed on Mrs. Seabright's explanation as Lloyd and I started out for the cars.

"Isn't it the custom to wait up all night on a first night for the morning papers?" he asked.

"For stage people it is. They like to know if they've still got their jobs the next day."

"That's one thing we needn't worry, about, eh? The Finchley Stores will pay the bill as long as we want them to. I understand the financial arrangements with you are satisfactory?"

"Quite satisfactory."

"How'd you happen to be in Washington at exactly the right moment for us?"

"Pure accident. This was the only place I could get a job when I got out of the Army."

"I suppose New York is really the radio center of the country. Martha tells me you were doing a show there before the war. Is that your home?"

"No, my home's in Cleveland. I had several local station jobs there before I made New York."

I heard him take a deep breath. "Smell the night. It's good to get out in the fresh air after all that—I loathe big parties." His tone turned confidential. "A few people in for dinner and some good solid talk afterward is my preference. That's one thing wrong with Washington—too many big social shindigs. You get so you're transacting half your business at parties. And if you are to stay away you find that pretty soon you're out of everything. That's why I bought our place in the country last summer. It's a half-hour away from the District, but I like it. As soon as we can get materials I'm going to build a stable and move my horses out there. They're all the company I need. Of course Alice doesn't see it that way."

He went on chatting busily as we approached my car. I looked at him in the light from the street lamp. He was wearing a topcoat and a stiff homburg-style hat. The fair hair gleamed white beneath it. His face no longer reflected the frank good nature I had grown used to seeing on it but was twisted now into an irate frown (I presumed at Alice). Somehow, though this picture he was painting of himself as a simple man of bucolic tastes didn't convince me, it didn't go with his terrific yen for the public spotlight. Maybe it was all part of a legend he was building up around himself—the gay playboy days were over, and from them was supposed to be emerging the thinking and unspoiled man of the people. He had done his thinking well and hard—the things he said on the show proved that—but I didn't see how he was going to put over this new personality.

I speculated on whether Linzell, publicity-wise and foxy, had thought it up for him. Now they're tired of this Groton, Exeter, Ivy League type, I could hear him saying, especially out there on the plains. They want a rough-hewn man close to the good earth, close to the life they know. Now you're going to move to the country and you're going to keep out of night clubs and you're going to ask your wife to confine her drinking as much as possible to her own sitting room. . . .

We reached the Crosley. Separated from it by a driveway was a big green Lincoln sedan. The rest of the street
was deserted.

"That's mine right behind you," Lloyd said.

We shook hands and I got into my car. We were on a
light downhill incline, so I released the emergency brake
and let her coast while I lighted a cigarette. Just as I took
my first puff I heard all hell break loose with a terrific
crash, and instantaneously my chest was jammed into the
steering wheel and hammer blows of pain shot through
me. Then I felt the Crosley spinning around and across the
street, and with another crash it came to a jarring halt, its
right door crushed against a tree.

After some tugging and lifting and a few loud groans
on my part Lloyd and Martha's butler freed me from behind the wheel and carried me indoors.

"Good lord, I'm sorry," Lloyd kept saying. "Good lord,
what a damn fool I am. I'm terribly, terribly sorry, old
man."

"Oh, Mr. Pike." Tears dripped down Geraldine's cheeks
below her glasses. "Oh, Mr. Pike. Oh, Mr. Pike."

"How is that, sir? Is that comfortable, sir? Would you
like your coat off, sir?" the butler kept asking in an insistent respectful voice.

"Don't fool with his coat, man," Mrs. Seabright scold-
ed. "Go and get him a drink. Can't you see that's what he
needs, a good stiff drink?"

Martha didn't say anything. I saw her pale face as she
bent over me and her satin gown all streaked with dirt and
oil, and then I saw the way she was looking at me was different from all the other times; there was concern in her
eyes, and tenderness, and something else I was afraid to
try to name just then.

"Your dress is ruined," I said. "What happened?"

"I don't know, old man." Lloyd ran his hand over his eyes. "I didn't see you. I can't imagine how it happened, but I just started up and plowed right into you. It's a bit dark there, and I thought you had gone on down the street. Good lord"—he shook his head—"I'm terribly sorry. Are you all right? Would you like a doctor?"

The butler came with a glass, and Mrs. Seabright poured some whisky down my throat.

"He'll be all right now," she told them.

I moved my legs and arms gingerly, inhaled and ex-haled. "I think I'm all in one piece, anyway," I said, and then I looked at Geraldine. "Guess we'll have to go home in a cab."

"Oh, Mr. Pike," she cried. "Oh, Mr. Pike."

"Of course we'll take you home, Alec," said Lloyd, "and of course I'll see about having the car fixed."

"Is there enough of it left to fix?"

"It's not so bad except for the rear and the door. While you're waiting for it I want you to use my station wagon. I'll have it brought in to you tomorrow."

"Thanks a lot," I said, and then I glanced around to find Martha's face again, but she had straightened up and was lighting a cigarette. An instant later, when she put it between my lips, she seemed quite her old self, and whatever I had seen or thought I had seen on her face had vanished, and she was busy instructing Lloyd about the shortest route to my apartment. I gathered that Lloyd was used to depending on his chauffeur to get him around the city and didn't know much about the streets.

A good while later as we were driving home I began to wonder how Martha had known I lived at the Webster Apartments, since I wasn't listed in the telephone book and had never mentioned it to her. First Carlos and now she seemed to have all kinds of information that evening, but my head ached too much to figure it out. I lay back against the seat and stared at Lloyd's thick neck and wondered how the hell he could not have seen my car right there in front of him—and under a street light too.

Geraldine was sitting next to me, her coat drawn tight around her, looking very forgotten and lonely.

"Are you all right, Geraldine?" I asked.

"Oh, sure, Mr. Pike, I'm fine."

"Call me by my first name, won't you? I'm sorry our evening had to end this way."

"I'll remember this evening as long as I live, Alec."

I didn't know then that I'd remember it too—but for another reason.

11

I walked with a limp the next morning and sat on the drugstore stool in a peculiar twisted position while I ate my breakfast. The sleepy-eyed counter boy in his as yet unspotted white apron asked me what was wrong. I told him my car had been smashed up.

"Looking for a new one?" he asked. "There was an ad on the board when I left here yesterday. Someone wanted to sell a '39 Ford."

I told him mine could be fixed up, but as I was leaving I decided to take a look at the ad just in case. The bulletin board (supplied by the drugstore management, a neighborly service I had seen nowhere but in the Capital) was about two feet square and hung on the wall near the door. It was covered with small white cards asking or offering rooms, baby sitters, phonographs, and Russian lessons. Whoever had wanted to sell an automobile had found a buyer. The ad was gone.

"Well, you know how it is these days," the boy said. "It's no time to be smashing up a kiddie car even. I'll keep my eye peeled for you, Mr. Pike."

I thanked him and limped out to the street and hailed a taxi. I told the driver to take me to the corner of Gordon Street and Columbia Road. When we got there I asked him what he charged for waiting.

"Waiting?" he said. "You mean for you?"

"No, with me. I want to sit here until somebody comes out of that fourth red brick house over there, and then I want to follow her."

"I see what you mean," he said. He looked bleary-eyed and he needed a shave. "I been drivin' this hack all night. I'd jist as soon sit still and be paid fer it. How long will it be?"

"Might be an hour. Might be a lot less."

"O.K. with me, bud, if you want to pay fer it." He named the price. "Uh, what does this party you're waitin' fer look' like?" he asked. "Jist so's she doesn't git away without one of us seein' her."

"Blond. Very pretty. Legs."

"I see what you mean. You her husband?"

"No—just an—an interested friend."

"Now there's not going to be any rough stuff, is there?"

"God, no. Didn't you see how I got into this cab? I can hardly move."

"Oh," he said, "beat up?"

"In a way."

"Those blondes," he said, "anything can happen."

"I see what you mean," I said.

"Want to listen to Arthur Godfrey?"

"Sure."

He turned on the radio and we sat in silence while Godfrey mumbled over his commercials and played records. About twenty-five minutes later I saw Gloria run down the steps of her house to the curb and stand looking up the street. She wore a black suit with the jacket buttoned up tight and a sort of fancy little hat with a veil. The driver saw her too.

"That the one?"

"Yes."

"She must be lookin' fer a hack."

"Well, when she gets one follow it."

She got one in a minute or two and we trailed it all the way down to the Mayflower Hotel, where Gloria alighted and went inside. I paid my driver.

"Watch it, bud, watch it," he warned, and he drove away looking genuinely concerned.

I hobbled as fast as I could into the hotel and reached the lobby just in time to see Gloria far in the rear walking into the main dining room. I sat down and smoked a cigarette and watched all the people at the clerk's desk begging for rooms. Then I made a detour around a huge pile of bags belonging to people who had given up begging for rooms and took a walk past the main dining room. I didn't see Gloria at first, so on the way back I stopped at the entrance and looked in.

There she was sitting all by herself at a big table. There were a lot of silver-covered dishes in front of her, and she was eating her breakfast. A waiter came up and poured her coffee, then another waiter came up and uncovered her hot rolls. That breakfast with tip would come to over two dollars—but then I already knew she couldn't be living on a secretary's salary. Where did it all come from? Who provided her with the money it cost to play the little princess at the breakfast table?

I went back to the lobby and waited until Gloria reappeared and headed toward the Connecticut Avenue door. She walked, as usual, with her nose in the air and an expression of sleek contentment on her face from the expensive food all tucked in her tummy. The men waiting for rooms looked at her tight jacket and her ankles, and for a moment their miserable rooflessness was forgotten.

Outdoors she hesitated for a moment and then sauntered down the sidewalk. There are lots of small specialty shops on that part of the avenue and she studied each one intently. I did, too, keeping a safe distance behind her.

Finally she went into a store on the corner. That left me stymied in front of a lingerie shop. I had to keep staring at a pink bed jacket edged with maribou and a sheer black nightgown for so long that a saleswoman inside came up and stared back out at me as if I were one of those questionable characters who get a sex kick out of black chiffon. Finally Gloria came out carrying a small package and I was released from my horrible thralldom.

Our walk seemed to be over. She hailed a cab and gratefully I hailed one, too, and eased my bruised body gently down on its leather seat.

"Follow that car just ahead," I instructed the driver.

When he saw what was in it he turned around. He was an old man with white hair and wrinkles.

"Kinda early in the, morning, arent you, laddie?" He threw me a thoughtful leer and turned back to his driving.

This time we ended up at the Union Station, which was a break for an amateur like me, because in the crowds there I had less chance of being noticed. Gloria went straight to one of the ticket-window lines and took her place at its end. There was absolutely no way of my knowing or overhearing what kind of ticket she was going to buy, for when, or to what destination.

I went to a newsstand and got a *Washington Post* to hide me while I watched her. There was a short write-up of our broadcast on the front page and a review on the radio page. There was also a typical news photo of Martha and Lloyd and me in front of the mike with our mouths hanging moronically open. I read the very approving article, glancing up now and then over the paper's edge to see Gloria moving nearer and nearer to the window.

Suddenly I felt a hand clap me hard on the back. I let out a yelp of pain and rage.

"How's the old master today, huh?" demanded a familiar voice. It was Ralph Logan, my ex-boss, his plump face newly shaven and smelling of that he-man's lotion, an overnight bag in his hand. "Trying to lam out of town after the performance you put on last night?" I winced as he pumped my hand up and down.

"What was the matter with it, Mr. Logan? Didn't you like it?"

"I wouldn't like anything connected with M. Finchley."

"Aside from your personal prejudices, how was it?"

He puffed out his lower lip. "Not bad. Not bad. But couldn't you cut down her lines?"

"I didn't think she was particularly intrusive," I said coldly. I glanced toward Gloria. She had moved up to third in line.

"Say, what's the matter with you?" The plump face turned quizzical. "Falling for her?"

"I wouldn't put it that way."

"My boy, that's a dangerous tumble. Take it from me. She's only interested in people she can milk something out of. Soon as this passing fancy for radio is past—whiff"— his hand made a swift motion under my nose—"out you go. There's no future in That One."

"Thanks for the advice."

"But you're not having any?" He shrugged and looked at his watch. "If I didn't have to go up to New York to haggle over some old diamonds I'd stay and talk some sense into you. I'm a real friend of yours, whether you know it or not."

"As a real friend of mine, how did you like the show?" Gloria was second in line now. "I talked to a lot of people at Mrs. Finchley's house last night, but you're the first outside person I've seen."

"I'll tell you," he said, "that Seabright was a wizard. He carried the intelligent part of the thing. I can do without that lady columnist—that female Peeping Tom what's-her-name—and that M. Finchley patter, but I'll tune in next week to hear Seabright. And you, of course. No hard feelings for the way you walked out on us."

"Once you told me you'd know Mrs. Finchley's motive for putting on the show after you heard one broadcast. Well, what is it?"

"My boy, it's what it always was. She's bucking for President of the United States."

At that moment Gloria put a ticket into her purse and turned away from the window.

"So long, Mr. Logan," I said quickly, and I started off as fast as I could go on my wrenched leg.

"So long, sucker," I heard him call after me.

Then it was a race for the cabs again, and I thanked God that I was playing a tail in a part of the land where cabs are so plentiful. This time my driver neither leered at my instructions nor warned me about blondes. He kept quiet and did what I told him, and we took a nice drive down Pennsylvania Avenue and then cut across up to Sixteenth Street, where Gloria paid off her cab a few doors past the Statler Hotel.

I got out at a corner and watched her go up some steps into a three-story brownstone house that was apparently being used for offices. When she had disappeared I walked up to the house. Several brass plates were nailed beside the door: P. T. Richards, M.D., National Metal Society, League for Forest Preservation, Ridgehill Company, Louis Sandowsky, and Congressional Research, Inc. When I got inside the old-fashioned high-ceilinged hall I heard typewriters clacking through the closed doors. Could it be possible, I wondered, that the girl actually worked here? If so, where? In which office? I climbed up the stairs to the second floor and then on to the third floor, but no one was around, none of the doors were open. I went back to the first floor again and walked into the doctor's waiting room. A woman in a white starched uniform was at the desk.

"Do you have an appointment?" she asked.

"No," I said, "I'm looking for somebody. I wonder if you could give me some information. I'm looking for a young lady who works in this building, I think. Her name is Gloria Hart."

The nurse shook her head. "I don't recognize it. But I'm not much acquainted with the others around here. We're kept pretty busy and—"

"Maybe you've seen her. She's extremely pretty, blond curly hair, slender—"

The nurse shook her head again. "I'm sure I wouldn't know, sir."

Just then a man walked out of the inside office carrying his hat and a physician's little black bag. He was a man in his fifties, with steel-gray hair and steel-rimmed glasses and a distracted scientific expression on his face. He glanced at me inquiringly.

"This young man is trying to find someone who works in the building," the nurse told him, "a young lady named Hart."

The doctor shook his head and bent over the appointment book lying open on the desk.

"Extremely pretty," I said, "blond curly hair, wonderful legs—"

He lifted his head. "Oh, *that* girl!" he said. "She works for Ridgehill. Second floor, second door to the right."

I walked upstairs again and stood outside the door of the Ridgehill Company. Like the other doors in that house, it was huge, paneled-oak, and heavy. I could hear the low muffled sound of voices, the click-clack of the inevitable typewriters, and once a telephone bell rang. Now what? I thought. So she worked for the Ridgehill Company, whatever that was. For all my pains, I knew little more than I had known before. I stood there undecidedly, wondering if I dared go back and ask the doctor if he knew what the Ridgehill Company was.

At that instant someone turned the doorknob from the inside and I leaped away as if it had shot an electric current at me. Since I was unable to run down the steps I did the next best thing—hobbled to the end of the hall and stood there, ostensibly gazing out of the window.

The doorknob rattled and turned and I heard a man clear his voice and walk out. His footsteps approached the stairway and halted. At that moment I learned that that was no dumb song writer, the one who wrote "My Heart Stood Still." Then the footsteps started to come slowly and inexorably back toward me. I stared through the window at the people passing on the sidewalk. I saw the doctor, carrying his black bag, get into a parked coupe and I had to clench my fists to keep from beating them on the glass. What the hell is this? I asked myself. What is there to be afraid of?

"Why, Alec, hello," came a voice behind me.

I turned and faced Lloyd Seabright.

"Did you come for the station wagon?" he asked. "You remember I told you I'd have my man bring it to your apartment? You remember that, don't you?" he asked gently.

"Yes," I said. "Come to think of it, I do recall that now. I'm all mixed up today, I guess."

"Sorry it's so early," he said, "or we might have lunch—"

"Oh, I—I have an appointment in a few minutes anyway," I told him.

As we walked down the stairs together he asked me how I felt and I said a bit stiff but not bad at all.

When we got outside a chauffeur drove the green sedan up to the curb in front of us. Its front fenders were dented only slightly from last evening's accident. It had been the heavy double-barred shining bumpers which had done most of the damage to my little car.

"Drop you somewhere?" Lloyd asked.

"No, thanks. I'm going right over there—over to the Statler."

I did go over to the Statler too, I went into the bar and ordered a scotch and water and watched the waiters getting the tables ready for the day's drinking. My heart was still missing beats. So Gloria works for Lloyd Seabright, I told myself. So what's wrong with that? But when I lifted my glass my hand was so shaky that the drink spilled over. The bartender looked at the clock above the door which said 10:15 a.m. and then at me. Shaking his head with pity, he ran his cloth over the puddle I'd made.

12

On Wednesday I flew to Cleveland in a little over two hours. It took another hour to go by air-line limousine to the Statler Hotel and then by taxi to the apartment in Shaker Heights where my parents lived. I had plenty of time on the way to think about what I was going to do and its possible consequences. By the time I got through speaking my piece to the unknown Mrs. Benson I'd have set wheels in motion that I'd have a hard time stopping. Up until now I had been playing at being a Pinkerton dick—now the playing was turning serious. It was a little like one of those stimuli dreams when you think you're sun-bathing at Malibu and you wake up to find the house is on fire.

By the time my cab was inching along Cleveland's Carnegie Avenue I started getting stage fright about Stevie too. In the past three years (half his life) I'd seen him only twice, a couple of days at a time. Now I was going to take him back to live with me for a whole week. Now he was going to get a big dose of my company, and just because I was his father was no guarantee that he'd like it. I remembered how once as a kid I'd organized a neighborhood gang into a secret society. At the first meeting all the members had to prick their fingers and squeeze drops of blood into a glass as a symbol of everlasting fraternity. The blood was mingled already in Stevie and me, but would he tell me the coveted password? Would he let me into that exclusive clubhouse of his mind and heart?

I looked out at the amorphous row of buildings we passed, at the pet stores, the gas stations, the garages turned into florists' shops, the auto salesrooms, the dough-nut stands. The auto show windows were empty and the Warner and Swasey plant had a big brick addition, but beyond that nothing had changed much since I'd driven down this street every morning to work. It was still as ugly and helter-skelter as ever. I thought of my morning drive in the Capital, through the park and along the tranquil river, down Virginia Avenue toward the white arrow of the Washington Monument. I decided that the first day we got back I'd take Steve to the top of the monument.

As we waited for a red light at 100th Street I heard a tenor blaring an old song over the radio of the next car.

The song had been popular when I was courting Caroline and still in college and not a cent to my name. I used to hum it into her ear at the Mather prom, and the way she pressed her cheek to my chest and squeezed my hand misled me into believing she agreed. Well, maybe I had misled her, too, but I chose to put most of the blame onto the movies and the storybooks and my ignorance of that plentiful phenomenon—a little girl in a woman's body. Caroline had never lost her little girl's fondness for games. The hide-and-seek, chase-and-tag, tap-the-icebox mood of our courtship days was all she ever wanted. When we were married and that was over she had turned to another kind of gambling—a steady customer at every track and dive in town.

The light changed and we pulled away, but the song had started a train of thought in my head. Martha wasn't free. The way to Martha was expensive and difficult and fraught with obstacles like San Martin and Seabright and the even bigger one of her ambitions. I thought about her the rest of the ride home. What had made her what she was and how little I really knew about her and why I should have fallen in love with her.

I asked where Steve was when I got home.

"Caroline took him out to Euclid Beach," my mother said. "It's a farewell treat because he's going away."

"But it's after six. Didn't she know I'd be here by this time?"

"Yes, I told her."

Same old Caroline, I thought, same old tricks. She couldn't be indifferent to me if she was still trying to annoy me. At that moment I realized my own small triumph—I wasn't angry at her. I just didn't give a damn what she did any more.

"You don't have to leave tomorrow night, do you?" my father asked.

"I'm sorry," I told him, "but I've got that new show and it needs a lot of on-the-spot planning and work—"

"We listened Sunday night. We thought you did a splendid job. That Lloyd Seabright is one brilliant man, isn't he?" My father nodded approvingly. "We were very impressed with him. Our country needs more chaps like him—quick on the trigger and the right line on things."

"Isn't that Mrs. Finchley rather affected?" my mother asked.

"What makes you think so?"

"Just from listening to her talk one gets the idea she thinks she is awfully important."

"She's a rich woman," my father interrupted. "I remember reading her husband's obituary in the *Times*. He owned a chain of department stores."

"It's beyond me," said my mother, "how you can expect her parties to make a radio program."

"You enjoyed it, didn't you?"

"Well, it was interesting hearing all those celebrities, but . . ."

"She's the person who got them together, Mother. Underneath the lion-hunter act she's a wonderful person, believe me."

"Where did she get that roast beef and all those hams you were talking about?" my mother demanded. "We can't buy anything like that around here."

I began to understand the basis of her bad impression of Martha, and we got into a discussion of the meat supply in our respective cities and I told her about Rudy Jennings and *Gourmet Magazine*.

After we had talked awhile and Steve still hadn't come I looked up Mrs. Harvey Benson in the telephone book. She lived in an apartment hotel out on Euclid Avenue. I dialed the number.

Since Harvey had been an unprepossessing-looking chap I suppose I had visualized his wife as a similar type, mousy, with a Phi Beta Kappa key pinned to a flat bosom. At any rate, the voice that came over the wire announcing that "This is Winifred Benson" did not fit my bluestocking image. The voice sounded theatrical and warm and very familiar.

I explained to her who I was, and she said she'd heard all about me several times from Harvey.

"I'd like very much to see you as soon as possible," I told her. "I have something to discuss with you—something extremely urgent."

"Why, you make me very curious, Mr. Pike. Can't you give me a hint of what you're talking about?"

"I'm sorry. I'd rather wait until I see you."

"How is tomorrow at four? We can have cocktails here at my hotel. I'll wait for you in the bar."

I agreed and we said good-by.

As I was hanging up I heard voices and hurried into the living room. Caroline was there, looking handsome and eternally collegiate in one of those Best and Company plaid suits of hers and her usual red and pouting mouth. She was handing Stevie some trinkets. He hugged them to his chest as he turned to me.

"Here's your daddy," my father said.

"Go and kiss your daddy," my mother said.

"He doesn't have to," I said, "unless he wants to. Maybe he'd rather shake hands until we get better acquainted." Steve transferred his toys to one hand and held out the other. He had recently had a haircut, and under its fuzz his skull looked very round and vulnerable. I noticed for the first time, too, that his ears stood away from his head exactly the distance that good workmanlike ears should. In spite of my mental wrestling with it, that adult-to-child cliché slipped out.

"You've grown since I saw you last."

"Yes, I have, Grandpa measured me."

"And how's the reading coming along?"

"He can certainly read 'Deposit Coin Here,'" Caroline interrupted. "He gave all his business to the Penny Arcade—that's how he got the loot."

We stood there facing each other across the child of our long-forgotten intimacy, murmuring a few stilted pleasantries about this and that until she left.

Much later that night I lay awake listening to Stevie's light breathing in the twin bed next to mine. The street lamps on the boulevard below sent a faint glow into the room, and I could see the outlines of his possessions on the shelves: a starfish, a complicated Erector Set concoction, a row of books, a catcher's mitt.

If the program makes good, I thought, I can afford to get a housekeeper and an apartment and have Steve come to live with me. And then I thought I really had no business complaining about Caroline any longer, for now I was a bigger gambler than she had ever been, risking Steven and Martha and my career and everything I really wanted on a hunch of murder, on my memory of a dead man.

I have always figured that you can tell how a woman feels inside by the way she adorns herself outside. According to this theory, Winifred Benson's mood the next day at four was low. She had appealed for help to a flowered hat, a bright green dress, earrings, bracelets, mascara, and a strong dash of gardenia perfume. This eye-catching barrage was intended, I suppose, to obscure the fact that she herself was like a morning-after gardenia, faded at the edges, a little too fancy for daylight.

There was no daylight in the dim air-conditioned bar where we sat exchanging some small talk until our orders came. I kept trying to imagine her with Harvey, but the vision wouldn't quite focus—he had been such an owlish and solemn chap, so preoccupied with the world's ills. How could he have married this common-looking blond woman with the hard, desperate eyes? It was true she had a certain type of sex appeal and a wonderful controlled and husky voice and she didn't seem stupid by any means. I settled for the sex appeal. This left another big question— why had she married Harvey?

When our drinks were in front of us and the first swallow warming our throats, Mrs. Benson looked archly up at me. "Now then," she said, "what is it you wished to discuss with me, Mr. Pike?"

"Harvey. You knew him better than I, of course. Tell me—do you truthfully think he was the sort of chap to kill himself?"

She shrugged and moved her glass in little wet circles on the table top. "He loved me very much," she said. "I had written him a letter telling him I wanted a divorce, and I guess—well, naturally I wouldn't have written it if I'd known—I blame myself, Mr. Pike, deeply, terribly." Her voice broke and her eyelids made a sad descent. "I haven't had a moment free of self-reproach since—"

"What I'm going to suggest to you," I told her, "is that you needn't reproach yourself. Tell me, Mrs. Benson, did you receive any letters from Harvey saying how upset he was over your desire for a divorce? How do you know he was upset?"

She drew her brows together. "He never wrote me, but he drowned himself. I presume that's proof enough. But really—this is my personal—"

"I came here to tell you that I believe your husband did not drown himself but was murdered."

She put her glass down hard, and the drink spilled over and ran in little rivulets toward the edge of the table. The flowers on her hat quivered.

"You're crazy," she announced loudly, and her gaze swept over me, hunting for the mad gleam, the telltale twitch. "What makes you say such a thing?" she demanded, "Have you any proof of such a thing?"

"No. That's why I came to see you. I thought you might help me get the proof."

"Oh, it's utterly impossible!" She subsided somewhat and mopped at the table with her paper napkin. "Why would anyone want to murder Harvey?"

"Exactly. Once we find a motive, we'll know whose motive it was. Do you know of any enemies Harvey had? Had he ever told you or written you of being afraid or of thinking someone was after him?"

"Of course not. It's ridiculous. He was drowned. The Army held an inquest or something and declared it a suicide. Harvey had a motive, didn't he?"

"With all respect to you, Mrs. Benson, isn't it rather romantic to assume that he killed himself for love?"

"Before we go on with this fantastic discussion, Mr. Pike"—she leaned over the table and the gardenia scent lapped at my nostrils—"don't you think you owe me. some explanations? Would you tell me what you have to base these—these suspicions of yours on and why you have taken it upon yourself to come around asking questions about the way Harvey died?"

"That's fair enough, though you might find my answers unsatisfying." I lighted a cigarette. Here is that why again, I thought, and it isn't the last time it will come up, either. It would be convenient to have a standard answer, something sure and tidy to put in the blanks of these questionnaires. One word that sounded good, like "friendship" or "loyalty" or "justice." But none of these told the truth. I didn't know what the truth was.

"I'm afraid," I said finally, "that I can't answer your second question yet. Could we leave it that I don't like to see anyone get away with murder? As to where I got my suspicions—the answer is fifty per cent intuition, fifty per cent Gloria Hart. (She's a little girl I'll tell you about in a minute.) Intuition, I know, is supposed to be mainly a feminine faculty, but mine is very well developed. I trust it."

Mrs. Bensons lips curved. "Intuition! You accused me of being romantic. I accuse you of being mystic."

"However, Gloria is very, very real."

Then I told her how I'd run into Gloria, her jittery reactions at the mention of Harvey's name, our subsequent dinner date, her story of what had happened in Italy, and her warning to me.

"Well, there you have it," Mrs. Benson burst out. "If no one else was on that boat but Harvey and that Italian, he either jumped off or that Italian killed him."

"I don't believe Gloria's story that there was no one else on the boat. I don't believe anything she says. She's a mytho-maniac."

"But who *was* there? That ought to be easy enough to find out."

"How? Gloria, as I told you, won't give me the Italian's name. I've come to a dead end unless, as I hoped, you can tell me something. What about his letters? Didn't he write you of his projected visit to Fucino or was he going to be there?"

"Yes, I think he wrote me about it, but he didn't mention the names. The names wouldn't have meant anything to me."

"Do you have his letters? Was there anything in the effects they sent back to you, any papers or diaries?"

"No." She shook her head. "No, when Mr. Miller was in town inquiring about a story I went through everything. There were only official papers—nothing personal in them."

"Who is Mr. Miller?"

"Mr. Ronald Miller. He's a lawyer from Chicago. After Harvey died he came here to give me a check for two hundred dollars. Harvey had given it to him for a down payment on some radio stock, but the deal never went through. I didn't know anything about it until Mr. Miller came here with the money. While he was here he just sort of incidentally asked me about some story of Harvey's."

"What kind of a story?"

Mrs. Benson frowned. "He didn't know. Harvey was always working on all kinds of stories, naturally—that was his business. He'd have been a roaring success in the old muck-raker days."

"Why was this Mr. Miller inquiring about a story?"

"Goodness," she said, "quite a cross-examination, isn't it? Well, I don't know. Mr. Miller said something about

Harvey having asked him to follow up this story in case he didn't return from overseas."

"Then he did feel something might happen to him?"

She gave me a bland smile of pity. "But he didn't mean anything except the fortunes of war."

"When did he leave this country?"

"August 19, 1943."

"I asked you a few minutes ago if Harvey had ever spoken of being afraid of anything," I said slowly. "I don't think you're being honest with me."

She took a compact out of her bag and snapped it open. "I don't care what you think." She peered into the mirror and patted her hair. "Harvey loved me, I'm telling you, and he killed himself because he thought I was leaving him."

"Why were you leaving him?"

"Because he bored me: I only married him because I needed pull for a radio job. He wangled me the part of Melissa in *The Strange Life of Melissa and Mark*. I was Melissa for two years."

So that's why her voice had sounded familiar to me. I had known the script writer for that soap serial and had tuned in on it many times to see what he was doing with the show.

"Our writer finally got drafted," Mrs. Benson was saying, "and no one seemed to fit into his place. I've been unemployed ever since." She struck at her nose several times with a tiny puff. "Now don't act shocked about my motives," she said. "It's more or less the same thing you are doing—only maybe you won't have to marry that elegant Martha Finchley."

"What are you talking about?"

"Oh, newspaper syndicates are wonderful things, Mr. Pike. Even up here in the sticks we read 'Washington Carousel.' My advice to you is to forget about Harvey. You can't help him any. Just get on a plane and go back to Washington."

"On the contrary, I'm thinking of going to Chicago."

"O.K." She tucked her things into her bag and stood up. "Why should you take my advice? I'm not on the Mr. Anthony show—yet."

When she had left the bar I ordered another drink and tried to figure out what went on under Mrs. Benson's flowered hat. Somehow the fact that Harvey had been cheated out of love, had been married by a woman who wanted only to use him, made his death seem all the more heart-rending and horrible. One thing appeared certain—this widow of his wasn't going to be much help to me at present. How much did she really know? What was she keeping from me? How was I going to make her talk?

After a while I got weary of guessing at her angles and tie-ups. I ordered a third drink and started to think about Enid Hoyt and what she had put in her column about Martha and me and whether I should be glad or angry.

13

The waiting room in the offices of Janes, Pritchard, and Bing were apparently designed to keep from visitors the pedestrian fact that they had come to consult attorneys rather than to join the Knights of the Round Table. The round table itself, of heavy carved oak, stood in the center of a gory red carpet. Carved high-back chairs, their red velvet seats battened down by nailheads, lined the oak walls. There was a fake fireplace at one end of the room over which hung a gaudy and indeterminate coat of arms. Indeed the illusion of olde England was intruded upon only by a current copy of *Business Week* and a stuffed and mounted outsize muskellunge.

I was staring at this creature's evil picket-fence teeth when Mr. Ronald Miller's secretary appeared. She was a tall, well-bred-looking girl with shiny black hair pulled into a bun on her neck. Mr. Miller, she informed me in an elegant and faraway voice, had left for the day. I told her how anxious I was to see him. I told her that Mr. Lloyd Seabright had recommended Mr. Miller very highly and that I had some very important emergency business and that since Mr. Seabright had told me Mr. Miller was just the man I needed how could I get in touch with Mr. Miller?

The girl looked puzzled. "I wonder if you mean Mr. Janes?" she asked. "It's Mr. Janes who handles Mr. Seabright's work."

I'd have liked to kiss her for that information, but I merely shook my head and insisted it was Mr. Miller I had to reach immediately.

"Oh, Mr. Miller can't be reached," she announced. "I can make an appointment for you in the morning."

"But I've come all the way from Washington and I have to leave tonight."

"I'm sorry, sir, but I'm afraid it's impossible."

"It isn't impossible unless he's ill or out of the city. Is he?"

She didn't say a word, just smiled mysteriously. All right, I thought, she wants to play twenty questions.

"Would he be at his golf club, by any chance?" I asked her. It was like mentioning Seabright before, just a hunch, but this one worked too. Her hauteur crumpled. At Miss So-and-So's School for Secretaries there had been no course in what to say when the boss is playing golf. I pressed my advantage. "Listen, young lady," I said, "you just give me the name of the club and how to get there and I promise it will be all right with Mr. Miller. My business is about a mutual friend. He'd want to see me if he knew I was here."

It took me a couple of minutes to break her down. Without saying it, she seemed to want to get it over to me that her work was below her station, that she'd only gone to Miss So-and-So's instead of Miss Spence's because Daddy lost his money, and so forth. I also, for some tenuous reason, maybe the way she said his name, got the idea that she had a crush on Mr. Miller.

The club, she admitted finally, was the Greenoaks Country Club, situated, reasonably enough, in the suburb of Greenoaks. I could get there on the Northwestern Electric in about fifty-seven minutes. She consulted her refined gold wrist watch. "I'm afraid Mr. Miller will be on the course by the time you get there. Mr. Miller's a very ardent golfer." As I walked out I passed the muskellunge and glanced at the plaque tacked below it. "Caught by R. E. Miller," it said, "St. Lawrence River, August 19, 1943."

Quite a sportsman, this Mr. Miller!

He didn't look like one though. I was standing on the clubhouse terrace, when a waiter pointed Mr. Miller out to me as he came in sight with another man on the ninth green. He was a bald, gone-soft-and-fat fellow in his forties, deeply sunburned. I waited until the two of them had sunk their putts and the caddy had replaced the flag, then I called and hurried over to them.

When I got close to Mr. Miller I could see what, it was that might have attracted his secretary—his beaked nose, his full red lips and cool eyes gave him a quality both arrogant and brutal. He was regarding me with puzzlement.

"I want to apologize for this intrusion," I said to him. "I hope you'll pardon my trailing you out here, but I'm only in from Washington for today and I had to see you. My name is Alexander Pike and I am—I was—a friend of Harvey Benson's."

"Oh yes?" His expression didn't change. He held out his hand and I shook it. Then he introduced me to his partner. "This is Mr. Eddy, Mr. Pike." I shook hands with Mr. Eddy. "Well, now"—Mr. Miller gestured toward the terrace—"if you don't mind having a drink or two until we've finished our game I'll be glad to—"

I said, "I know this is presumptuous of me, but would you mind if I walked around a couple of holes with you? I have to get back to town to catch a plane for Cleveland."

"I understood you to say you were from Washington."

"Yes, I am. But I have some business in Cleveland on the way back." A vision of Mrs. Benson, the mascara, the earrings, the flowered hat and hard eyes, rose, I suspected, before both of us. He shrugged. "All right," he said. "It's all right with me, but—"

"Oh, sure, R. E.," said Mr. Eddy. "It's O.K. with me. The kind of game I play, this is probably my only chance to get a gallery." He chuckled as we walked to the tenth tee.

Miller whacked his ball a good two hundred and sixty yards.

"The guy's a regular machine," enthused Mr. Eddy. "A regular machine." He swung his own club and topped the ball. "Guess I lifted my head too soon, eh, R. E.?" he asked anxiously. The second time he topped the ball again and it rolled a reluctant hundred yards down the fairway.

"Well, you're not in any trouble on that one," Miller remarked generously.

We started after the balls.

"I give this guy a big hunk of business every year, Mr. Pike," said Mr. Eddy, "but I make him sweat for it out on the golf course."

When we had left him behind and were walking toward Miller's ball Miller said to me, "Now, Mr. Pike, what's on your mind?"

"Benson. He's been on my mind ever since he drowned himself in Italy last year. I just don't believe that he did."

"Oh?"

"Frankly I've taken it upon myself to do some investigating."

"I suppose that's a thankless task?"

"I don't think so. Especially not if it restores my peace of mind."

"You're—uh—you're disturbed about the suicide?"

"My theory is that Benson was onto something somebody didn't want known and was put out of the way for it. That's why I've come to see you, Mr. Miller." Over the cool eyes his sun-bleached eyebrows lifted. "Mrs. Benson told me yesterday about your visit to Cleveland and that you were looking for some story Harvey had instructed you to take over for him."

"Oh. Oh yes, I recall that now." He squinted toward the horizon, as if that recollection was very far away. "Oh yes, of course. Mrs. Benson told you I'd been to see her."

We had reached his ball. He stepped up to it and knocked it terrifically hard and straight. After a moment we saw a white dot appear on the edge of the green. Mr. Eddy was still hacking his way behind us.

"About that story of Harvey's," I began as we walked on.

"I don't imagine that one could be the one you're looking for. I don't think it was of much importance."

"Then you don't know what it was about?"

"I can't say. I never found it, you know."

"But didn't Harvey tell you something about it when he asked—"

"As a matter of fact, he didn't," Mr. Miller's red lips stretched in a rueful smile. "He merely dropped the word that he had something like that on his mind and would like to have it followed up. I forgot all about it until I heard of his passing. Then it weighed on my conscience— you know how that is. I thought I'd better make the gesture of trying to find it. I didn't expect any luck and, as his widow probably told you, I didn't have any."

He seemed to be treating the whole matter with exaggerated casualness. I wondered how Harvey had happened to confide in this muscle-man type, anyway. I tried to pump him some more.

"When did Harvey tell you about this mysterious story?" I asked.

"It was just before he sailed. I happened to be in New York the very night before, in fact, and we had a talk. That accounts for it, you know. He was nervous and jumpy— submarines and all—and I just happened to be there to talk to." We halted our conversation then because Miller was about to putt. He got ready for it solemnly, squatting on the ground to line it up first, and then standing Indian-still as he addressed the ball. I had stopped talking, but I hadn't stopped thinking. What I was thinking about was the muskellunge hanging back there in the office. August 19, 1943, the day Miller caught the muskie in the St. Lawrence, was, Mrs. Benson had told me, the day that Harvey had sailed with his unit for North Africa.

Miller swung his putter. His ball rolled neatly over the smooth turf and into its hole.

"My God," said Mr. Eddy, "the man's a regular machine."

We sat down on a bench at the eleventh tee and waited for a foursome ahead of us to move along up the fairway. I took my wallet out of my pocket and flipped it open. Beneath its cellophane window was a snapshot of two smiling men in uniform. I showed it to Miller.

"Harvey sent me this," I explained. "It was taken just before he died. Doesn't look very depressed there, does he?"

"Nope." Miller gazed at the picture. "Can't say he does there." His blue eyes glinted up at me. "But just because a fellow grins when he's facing a camera doesn't mean that he feels that way inside, would you say?"

"Nope." I tucked the wallet away.

The foursome had reached the green, and Mr. Miller teed up his ball. I watched him get ready to drive, his thick buttocks moving from side to side as he fixed his stance, the club slender as a wand beneath his heavy arms. I knew he was going to hit that ball very far. He could do some things well, it was obvious: play golf, land a big fish (large North American pike sometimes weighing sixty to eighty pounds). But now the tables were turned. A Pike had baited him and hooked him too. Harvey hadn't been in that snapshot in my wallet. It was a picture of two other guys. Mr. Miller had never laid eyes on Harvey.

On the plane to Cleveland I took an old envelope and a pencil out of my pocket and wrote down on it: "The firm of Janes, Pritchard, and Bing, of which Mr. R. E. Miller is a member, represents Lloyd Seabright." Then underneath that, one item to a line, I wrote:

> Gloria Hart was with Harvey Benson the night he died.
> Miller tried to get access to Harvey's private papers.
> Gloria Hart works for Lloyd Seabright.

One, two, three, four, there it was in black and white, and what was it all about? Harvey was connected with Gloria and Miller, Seabright was connected with Gloria and Miller. Couldn't it follow that Harvey and Seabright were connected too?

Suddenly I had a feeling in my stomach as if the plane had dived a thousand feet. Maybe Harvey's story was about Seabright! Maybe he had dug up something really fatal to that big ambition. My God, I whispered to myself, and I heard again the crash of the green Lincoln into the rear of my Crosley. I felt myself spinning again and again; my chest was stabbed with pain where I'd jammed it against the steering wheel. Gloria Hart told Seabright what I was after and he didn't like that. For some good reason he didn't like that and he ran into me on purpose—tried to kill me. Mentally I fingered all the pieces and attempted to fit them together.

The key, I felt sure, lay in Seabright's character. I recalled vividly the three or four times I had been with him, the distinguished face, the good voice, the good manners. So he wanted a public career, starting at the top—Senator Seabright. He'd never get it if he were a candidate for election, if he had to run for it on the basis of his qualifications. He was a good polo player, a perfect country gentleman—but why did he deserve the honor of high office? What kind of service was he fitted to perform? He hadn't lived in his own state for years. He hadn't ever lived with or near the voters of his state. Why should he represent them? I wondered why Martha was supporting him so avidly—Martha Finchley, the king maker. How much did she really know about him? There was one question I needed answered. Seabright had wangled himself a job abroad for the State Department during the war. Had he been to Italy? Had it been in the third week of September 1944, the week Harvey Benson was drowned?

I had wired my parents to bring Steve to the airport, as I got in from Chicago just a half-hour before the plane to Washington departed. I found them in the main lounge, the little boy, very scrubbed and solemn, sitting stiffly in a big leather chair.

"He hasn't eaten all day," my mother said. "I told him you'd leave him home if he didn't eat something."

"Why did you say that?" I demanded angrily. "I'd do no such thing. I wouldn't leave him behind for anything in the world."

"Is that the way to talk to your mother?" my father asked. "She was thinking of the boy's own good."

"I don't want her threatening him."

My mother sniffed. "Everything I do is wrong," she said.

I put my arm around her. "I'm sorry, Mother—it's just that I know he was too excited to eat. Anyway, we'll get dinner on the plane." I looked at the big clock over the door. "I've got one call to make," I told them. "Be back in a few minutes."

I dialed Mrs. Benson's number. The phone rang and rang. When she answered it she sounded a bit high. Through the earpiece I heard a radio playing and the sound of voices.

"Sorry to disturb a party," I said.

"Oh. It's Dick Deadeye. What do you want?"

"The same thing I wanted yesterday—information."

"You'll get the same thing you got yesterday—nothing"

"Now listen here, Mrs. Benson," I said with what I hoped was an undertone of menace. "I think you'd better spend a little more time and thought on the subject. I've just come back from Chicago, from seeing that very fishy character, R. E. Miller."

"Well?"

"He wasn't your husband's attorney. He never even laid eyes on your husband. Apparently that two-hundred-dollar check was all fixed up in order to get access to Harvey's papers through you. I advise you to tell me now what story he wanted and what this whole business is all about. Because if you don't I'm going to find out anyway, and it may not look so good when it gets out that you've kept the thing to yourself."

"May not look so good to who?" she asked. "Deadeye, you bore me. Good-by now."

"Wait a minute. If you change your mind and want to reach me I live at the Webster Apartments—"

I heard the receiver click and I was cut off.

When we were in the air Steve said, "The cars down on the road look just like my toy cars at home."

"Are you going to miss home?"

"Oh no. Not for just one week."

"Suppose it was more than a week? Suppose you were to stay in Washington and live with me always?"

"Have you a bed for me?"

"Yes, I have a bed."

"Would there be a place to put my toys?"

"We could get some shelves."

"Oh, look!" he cried. "That cloud is like one of Mother's fuzzy sweaters."

"You wouldn't see your mother very much," I warned him. "You'd have to leave all your friends and go to a new school." He was regarding me with big thoughtful eyes. "Of course there'd be some good things about coming to live with me. We'd have lots of fun together. There're so many interesting things to see and do in Washington."

His sober little boy's mind thought about that for a minute.

"The thing I'd like best," I went on carefully, "would be coming home from work every day and finding you to talk to. The way it is now, I get so lonesome I talk to your picture."

He gave me a swift grin. "What do you say, Dad?"

"Sometimes I tell you about the paddle boats we could ride in the Tidal Basin, or about the wonderful performing brown bears at the zoo, or how it is to ride on the little train in the basement of the Capitol." His face was glowing and I went on shamelessly, "Or about the famous Army generals I see on the street, with four stars on their shoulders and chests full of medals."

The stewardess came just then with our dinner trays and our discussion was halted. But even after we'd eaten Steve didn't go on with it. He curled up with his face to the window and stared at the sky. I didn't have the courage to press him. Besides, it was just talk—I couldn't afford a household of my own for a long while yet. This unpleasant fact turned my thoughts around to the new show and its star and backer, Lloyd Seabright. I went over the details of the auto accident again, and again I was convinced that it had been no accident. What could Harvey have dug up about Seabright? I asked myself. What made Lloyd Seabright tick?

"Dad," Steve said suddenly.

"Yes?"

"Do you leave the lights on all night in your bath-room?"

"Why, yes," I said, "I guess so. Sure I do."

"Well, then"—he gave me a long sweet smile—"then I'd like to come and live with you always, Dad."

14

On Sunday night, just before I started out for Martha's house, Geraldine Hudock called to tell me Gloria had left town.

"Have you any idea where she went?" I asked.

"No. She wouldn't tell me. She said she'd write when she could. She certainly put on the mystery act. I think there's something funny about it."

"How do you mean?"

"Did you ever find out where she worked?"

"No. Not for sure."

"I think this trip is connected up with wherever she works. She said it was on business."

"I see. And you don't have any way of tracing her? Where'd she say to send her mail?"

"She didn't say."

"Well," I said, "the way my luck's been going recently, this is just what I might expect."

"Oh, Mr. Pike. How've you been feeling since the accident?"

"I was stiff the day after. I'm fine now."

"Have you found out anything more, about that Mr. Benson?"

"Not much. I tell you what, Geraldine, you can help if you'll keep me informed about any line you get on Gloria's whereabouts."

"Sure. I'll call you right away. And good luck tonight. I'll be listening."

When she rang off I showed Stevie how to dial Martha's number if he needed me after he went to bed.

Our second broadcast went off perfectly, and during the actual show I was all right. I fell into my master of ceremonies role, and Seabright was just part of the act to manipulate for the best dramatic effect. But when we signed off I realized that I was streaming with nervous perspiration and weak with hate. A waiter offered me a plate piled with food, but I couldn't eat. I don't know how I got through the next few hours, smiling when I was smiled at, talking when I was talked to, saying thanks when I was complimented on the performance. I kept as far away from Seabright as possible, always leaving a room as soon as he entered it. Whenever I heard his voice I felt my fists clench in my pockets, and my face color with rage. I was afraid—I don't know of what exactly—of losing control of myself, perhaps.

The last guest left Martha's house at twelve-thirty. She had seen them all to the door, and when she came upstairs I was standing stupidly in the center of the room while the servants passed back and forth and around me, cleaning up.

Martha said, "Could I induce you to come outside to look at the moon?"

"I was outside. There is no moon."

"Come on anyway. We can't talk in here."

I followed her downstairs again and out onto the terrace. She stood on the edge of it, raising her arms like slender branches to the black sky. Without toning she said, "You're in a bad mood tonight, aren't you, Alec? At first I thought you had mike nerves, but even after everything went off so well you were carrying a jumbo-sized chip on your shoulder. Tell me, what's the matter?"

"All right. There is something I'd like to discuss with you."

"Could we possibly discuss it at your apartment? To make sure we won't be interrupted?" She glanced around at the empty chair where Carlos had sat the week before.

"Oh, he!" I looked down at her. "Does he come back every night?"

"He usually wants a nightcap."

"Even when he's not invited?"

"Even when he's not invited."

"Rotten-mannered chap, isn't he?"

"Why don't you like him?"

"I like him. That hot-eyed Latin type just doesn't arouse me."

"Then come on. Let's go over to your apartment."

"But it isn't very comfortable. I mean—"

"You're always hinting," she said, "that all I know about Washington is S Street and Massachusetts Park. Why don't you show me how the other half lives? It's an experience I ought to have." She gave me a soft sidelong glance, and then we walked back through the house and she took a jacket out of a closet. We went out the front door and got into the station wagon.

"When will your car be ready?" she asked.

"In about two weeks if I'm lucky. I'm thinking of trading it in for an armored tank."

"Did the accident make you that jumpy?"

I drove the wagon up the street until we were at the place where my Crosley had been hit. "Plenty of light here, isn't there?"

"Seems to be."

"Don't you find it curious that Lloyd couldn't see me that night?"

"It was dreadful carelessness. He was probably think-ing about something else—not paying any attention. You know how people suddenly get blind spots."

"And if he'd accidentally killed me there'd have been no penalty. Of course my estate could have sued for negli-gence, but what good would that do me? I'd be dead, peri-od. Lloyd Seabright would be alive and free, exclamation point." I shifted into third and drove on down the street toward Connecticut Avenue. "Does it add up to anything for you?" I asked curtly.

"He ought to pay more attention to where he's going after this," she murmured.

"Is that all?"

"What do you mean?"

I didn't answer. I jammed my foot viciously down on the gas and we sped up Connecticut Avenue.

She stood aside at the door until I walked into the black room and switched on a lamp. Then she tossed her jacket over a chair and looked around. "Well," she said, "it has personality. A certain dejected kind of personality. How did you happen to find it?"

"Through a grapevine. It belongs to a civil service clerk named Pearse whose wife walked out on him. From what the girls at the switchboard tell me, Mr. Pearse never got a word in during their scraps. That was the only way he had of expressing himself." I pointed to the fussily scrolled sign over the telephone. "There's another one in my bed-room, four lines entitled *Remembering.*"

"A sad story."

"It's left its mark too. The place is like an old battle-field reeking of defeat." As Martha started to cross the room I turned and blocked her way. "However," I said, "I'm not going to let it affect me."

Her chin was tilted up to me. Below it I saw her white throat and the pulse beating at its base and then the deep V of her dress glittering where the sequins caught the light. I felt her hands moving upward along my arms.

"Poor Carlos," she said, "how he hates to miss his nightcap."

"Is that what you're thinking about?"

"No."

"What are you thinking about?"

Her hands gripped my shoulders, and I felt the warmth and smoothness of her lips beneath mine, and their command and insistence too.

"Remembering?" she whispered. "Show me how he got remembering into four lines."

"Darling, listen," Martha was saying. "Darling, listen. What was that?" Her voice was far away; as if she were calling me from the bottom of a long flight of stairs. "Wake up, darling," Martha was saying, "listen." Her voice was getting nearer, as if she were running up the stairs toward me. "Listen," she said again, and her voice was like a bell in my ear. I opened my eyes.

"Now you can tell me I'm out of my mind. It seems to me someone's been calling right from the next room."

"Dad, Dad, Daddy," came the voice.

"You didn't hear anything, did you?" asked Martha.

"Daddy," the voice called again.

"Jesus Christ," I said loudly.

Steve wanted a drink of water. "Why didn't you answer me, Dad?" His eyelids drooped. "I called you for such a long time."

"I'm sorry, Steve, the door was closed."

"When I come to live with you will you leave the door open always, Dad?"

"Sure, Steve. Sure I will."

When I came back with his drink he was asleep, his small stubby profile pressed into the pillow. I'd forgotten that anyone could look so trusting.

Martha was dressed and sitting in the living room, in the large chair with the torn cushion, smoking a cigarette.

"Who is that, darling?" she asked pleasantly.

"My son. I brought him back from Cleveland to spend a week before school begins. I completely forgot about him. Makes me feel like a traitor."

"I remember now. You did say you'd been married. Tell me about it."

"I married a girl I knew in college. It was one of those things that's worn out before it begins, but neither of us knew how to back out. Lots of silly things like habit and what people might think propelled us into it. It was all over before I went into the Army. Steven will be seven years old soon."

"What was his mother like?"

"Spoiled and good-looking. She said I suffocated her personality. She was crazy about gambling the money we didn't have. I suppose we might get along better now since I've become a gambler myself."

"How do you mean?"

"That was what I meant to discuss with you tonight before we—got sidetracked."

She leaned her head against the back of the chair, her eyes half closed, and smiling. "That's one thing I haven't heard it called before."

I got myself a cigarette and sat down on the couch opposite her.

"All right, don't look so grim, darling," Martha said. "Tell me about it. How are you gambling?"

"First answer one question for me. Lloyd Seabright was in Italy on some State Department business during the war, wasn't he?"

"What's Lloyd got to do with it?"

"When was he in Italy?"

"Heavens, all this mystery! He was there the same time I was."

"Oh. Then he was the reason you had to be in Rome."

"Not at all. It was a delightful coincidence. Naturally there were all sorts of doors opened to Lloyd that might have been closed to me. He took me around and I was able to do some very exciting columns on Italy. Everyone said they were my best ones."

"And while going around with Lloyd did you ever meet an Italian gentleman who owned a villa at Lake Fucino?"

"I wouldn't know, unless you told me his name. But what are you driving at? You haven't yet told me how you are gambling."

"I'm risking my life on the hunch that Seabright's a ruthless, no-good bastard who stops at nothing to get what he wants—not even murder."

I remember how she was sitting relaxed in her chair, the lamplight making a sparkle here and there on her dress, the cigarette loose in her fingers. She stayed that way too. Only her eyes and her voice turned hard and furious.

"Explain, please," she said slowly.

"It's a long story, Martha. I know only parts of it. I make up other parts of it. I'm gambling that I'm right. That when the rest of the story comes to light the facts will be what I imagine them to be."

"Tell me the story, but please be sure to indicate which parts are flights of fancy, will you?"

"I wish I knew what Lloyd Seabright means to you. Why his ambitions mean so much to you."

"Would knowing that change your opinion of him?"

"No, but—"

"Then I don't see that it serves any purpose to explain that to you now."

Faintly in the next apartment a clock chimed twice as I began to tell her about Harvey Benson, the same story I

had told Mrs. Benson only a week before. Except to chain-
light one cigarette after another, Martha didn't move all
the time I was speaking. But when I came to the part about
following Gloria and finding she worked for Seabright,
Martha made an exclamation of impatience.

"Wait," I said, "wait. There's lots more. The next thing
that happened was that Lloyd ran into me with his Lincoln. You were there. I don't have to tell you the details.
Then you remember I told you I had to be out of town for
a day or two but I didn't tell you I was going to Cleveland because there was no point in making my movements
known just in case anyone was intensely interested. In
Cleveland I interviewed the Widow Benson, a tough dame
whose ego had flourished on the story that her husband
killed himself for love of her. What I needed, you see,
was a motive. Why would anybody kill Harvey? My theory
was that he'd dug up some kind of a story that might be
embarrassing to someone. He was completely fearless and
incorruptible, and if he had gotten onto some information
that should be made public nothing could have stopped
him from spilling it—except death."

"Well, what did his wife say?" asked Martha. "Did you
find there was any such story?"

"See, it's interesting, isn't it? It makes you want to go
along and find out more. That's just the way it worked
with me. No, I didn't find out that any such story existed from Winifred Benson, though she certainly knew
a lot more than she told me. But I found out a curious
thing. A man named Miller, a Chicago lawyer, had already
been to see Mrs. Benson and asked the same question. He
had more reason than I, since he claimed he was Benson's
attorney and that Benson had even asked him to follow up
on a certain story, still nameless, in case anything prevent-
ed Benson from returning. This bears out my theory that

such a story exists, doesn't it? However, something very curious turned up."

"Curious! Strange! Queer!" Martha burst out. "Can't you talk without adjectives? Can't you let the facts stand by themselves. You're not giving a *Teller of Tales* broadcast, you know."

"What turned up," I continued, "is that I went to Chicago and found that the firm with which Miller is connected also does work for Lloyd Seabright."

"That sounds perfectly logical and ordinary to me. What is the firm's name?"

"Janes, Pritchard, and Bing. Ever hear of it?"

She shrugged. "I may have. They may do some work for Lloyd. I know they're not his chief counsel."

"What isn't logical and ordinary," I said, "was that Miller, far from being Benson's attorney or entrusted with any story of Benson's, had never laid eyes on Benson."

"Then the Widow was lying."

"No, Miller was lying. When I showed him a picture of two men from my division and told him one was Harvey Benson he didn't know the difference."

I told her how I'd gone back to Cleveland to get Steven and my telephone conversation with Mrs. Benson. "I have an idea," I said, "that I'm going to hear from her, that she knows more than she told me. It's been three days, but I still think she'll come through. Want a drink?"

She nodded. I went into the kitchen and got the ice and whisky and a box of cheese crackers, and we sat there drinking thirstily, both very wide awake, though it would soon be dawn.

"Why don't you say something?" I asked her.

"You haven't finished. You haven't yet told me the parts of the story you've imagined."

"That should be obvious."

"But I want to hear you say it."

"I imagine that the story Harvey Benson dug up was about Lloyd Seabright. I imagine that Lloyd found it out and had someone kill Harvey."

"But how? How?"

"He was in Italy at the time. Maybe he was even on that boat with Harvey. Gloria certainly was. I'd make another effort to get it out of her, but she's disappeared, by the way."

"Disappeared?"

"Spirited away. Gone. Vanished. Lloyd saw to that. He should have—she was a dumb babe. I imagine Lloyd got the Janes firm to try to get any further evidence that might be lying around in letters to Mrs. Benson, et cetera. I imagine Lloyd is worried about me and would like to shut me up for good."

"My God, but it's preposterous!" She brought her fist down on the arm of the chair. "How can you possibly imagine that a man like Lloyd Seabright would—would want to kill anyone? And just what kind of a story about Lloyd do you think there is? A skeleton in the closet? An insane grandmother or a bastard offspring?"

"Whatever it is, I think it might halt his precious career. It would certainly prevent him from getting that seat in the Senate he's after. It might, if he were in it as deeply as I figure, lead him to a hotter seat."

She stood up and walked over to the fireplace. Mr. Pearse's weather indicator, a little ugly plastic house officially called a "Weather Wizard," was on the mantel, and the boy and girl figures meaning tomorrow would be a nice day had come out of the door. Martha flicked her finger absent-mindedly at them, and they teetered back and forth with the witch figure meaning rain.

"You don't know Lloyd. I do," she said evenly. "I know him as well as one human being can know another. People like Lloyd don't commit criminal acts like that."

"Why not? Even a millionaire gets desperate. There's no such thing as a criminal class."

"But you haven't any proof. Not the slightest fragment of evidence." Her finger snapped again at the small figures, and they swung madly again through their door.

"Not yet I haven't. But I'm trying my damnedest to get some. Don't do that, you'll break that thing."

She turned around, her eyes blazing. "So I'll break your toy, eh? That's what you are, infantile—juvenile. Why, you haven't grown up yet! You're still playing games; you're still acting out pulp stories. Why don't you buy yourself a bloodhound and a bottle of invisible ink and really have some fun?" She stamped over to the telephone. "I'm going to call a taxi."

"I'll drive you home."

"Oh no, you won't."

After she'd phoned the cab I said, "Why are you so angry and upset? If what I said is really preposterous there's no need to worry, is there?"

"It's not because I'm worried," she flung at me from the door; "it's because this is the first time I've ever felt like anybody's mother!"

"Don't slam that," I warned. "The neighbors—"

The door crashed closed behind her.

I went back to bed and smoked a cigarette. That was a fine row, I thought; everybody on the floor must have heard us. Then in the faint light of dawn coming through the windows I saw that she had left her little black evening bag on the bureau. She'd been here. She'd really been here. That was what mattered. Ah, I thought, to hell with the neighbors. . . .

15

"Well, Mr. Pike," said Frances Rhodes when I came in the next day just before six, "Ah'm certainly glad to see you're home!" She handed me three white telephone slips. "That woman called a lot more times, too, but Ah got tired of writin' it down."

I glanced at the papers in my hand. They all said the same thing; "Please phone Mrs. Winifred Benson, Mayflower Hotel." She was here. She had come when the most I had dared hope for was a long-distance call.

"She sure is real anxious to hear from you, Mr. Pike," Frances remarked.

"Naturally," I said, and my heart was beating as if I'd just seen a long shot first across the finish line. "All my women are like that."

She tossed her heavy dark mane. "Some of us try to be subtle about it, though."

"Look, Frances, put the call in for me, will you? I'll take it upstairs."

When I opened the door the telephone was ringing. I sprinted across the room and picked it up.

"Hello, Mr. Pike," said that familiar husky voice. "I'm glad you received my message at last. I'm in town only for tonight and I want to see you."

"Will you have dinner with me?"

"Oh? Well—all right, I—I guess that would be all right. I want to talk to you."

"How soon can I pick you up?"

"At seven, say—in the lobby."

"Fine. We'll have dinner at the hotel."

I suppose we could have had dinner at the hotel if we'd waited a half-hour in line, but we were anxious to sit down to a conversation important to both of us, and the crowds milling about the entrance to the cocktail lounge and dining room were discouraging.

"There's a new Russian place across the street," I said to Mrs. Benson. "Rather on the night-club side, I think, but we could try it."

She was wearing a navy blue suit and a hat with a white bird intricately made of feathers perched forward on its brim. The bird bobbed as she nodded in agreement. We started out, and I noticed that a man and another couple who were waiting had the same idea. They crossed the street and arrived at the door of the new place just behind us. Inside we found the usual setup: soft lights, murals of gay Russians in fur hats and tunics, a small orchestra, and a big crowd. The only table we could get was on the dance floor, just next to the musicians' platform.

I hesitated for a moment, wondering if we should go out and try to hunt down a quieter place, but Mrs. Benson wanted to stay. "We'll have to wait anywhere else we go," she said. "Maybe they won't play too loud."

When we ordered dinner I noticed she seemed nervous and less sure of herself than when I'd seen her first, and I wondered what had happened to make her decide to come and see me.

Reading my thoughts, she asked, "Are you surprised that I'm here?"

"I'm glad you're here. I need your help. Harvey needs your help."

Her lips twitched. "What can help him now? He's dead. Do you really believe anything makes any difference to a corpse?" Her eyes scanned my face. "I don't suppose I'll ever find out what makes you tick, Mr. Pike, but I'm willing to reveal my own inner processes. I came to see you because—well—because I'm frightened. Someone ransacked my apartment the day after you were in Cleveland. I've had a feeling I'm being watched." She glanced swiftly around. "I want to be rid of it, whatever it is," she said vehemently. "I—I can't stand this—persecution." Suddenly her face crumpled and she covered it with her hand. "I can't stand it," she sobbed. "I'm afraid to be alone. I keep thinking someone's following me."

I waited until she got herself under control.

"Who do you think it can be? Who is so interested in your movements?"

"It must be the—the people who were after Harvey—"

"Then there were—"

"That's what you said, didn't you?" she interrupted defiantly. "You're the one who told me all this gangster stuff about Harvey being murdered and so forth. If you hadn't come along stirring up trouble everything would be all right. I'd be all right."

"Are you sure of that? Wouldn't there have been at least a pang of conscience, knowing—

"You're a sententious bastard, aren't you? What I'd like to know is what you're getting out of all this. Don't tell me your reward is nothing but a clear conscience. I've lived too long for that sort of talk." She leaned over the table. "It's been my experience that in this world people look out for Number One." She tapped her chest. On her hat the white bird, symbol of innocence, bobbed incongruously. "But I didn't come down here to tell you my philosophy of life."

"Skip it, Mrs. Benson. What did you come down here to tell me?"

She glanced nervously once more at the crowded, shuffling dancers near us and then drew her chair closer to the table and bent toward me again.

"You've heard of the American Challengers, haven't you?"

"Sure. I've read about them. That's the fascist organization that used to make so much noise before the war, isn't it?"

"That's the one. Their isolationist line didn't go down so well when we got into the war, so they ran for cover. But they never really closed up shop. They were busy preparing to go back into business when the war ended. I guess they're at it already—there was something in the papers about a big rally they held in Chicago. They claim they want to purge Congress of all the men who don't believe in the American way of life. You know that old song and dance. Anyway, a friend of Harvey's became member of the group to get all the dope. He joined the marines later, but not until after he'd given Harvey a good lead. Harvey dug the rest out himself. Now you—you had some contact with the firm of Janes, Pritchard, and Bing—"

"I have."

"Janes is Lionel Janes, a fairly steady joiner of crackpot clubs. A story on him would be just a story. He's not important enough to be news. Besides, Harvey was convinced he was definitely the implement of somebody else "

"Then when Miller came to you with that two hundred dollars—then you knew all the time that Miller was not and never had been Harvey's attorney."

"Sure I did—but why should I let on to him? If they wanted to tell me a fairy story it was all right with me, and the two hundred dollars came in handy. I'm no reformer."

"Then why did you mention Miller to me? Why did you tell me about his coming to see you and so forth?"

"I was curious to see what you'd do. If you wanted to go on playing cops and robbers it was nothing to me, just so you left me out of it. I'm here now only because I'm desperate; I'm afraid of Miller and the rest of them. However, let me get back to my story—since I presume that you are interested in that and not in my personal motives."

"That's right, Mrs. Benson."

"Well, Harvey finally found out who was behind Janes. Don't ask me how. He was a regular bloodhound, as you know. Now who do you think was giving Janes all the money that the Challengers needed, with the promise of a lot more after the war? That personality boy on your show—that Lloyd Seabright!"

I gripped the table. Was she sure?

She raised her eyebrows. "I thought you knew Harvey."

"I'm sorry. But why didn't Harvey break the story when he got it?"

"He certainly should have, but that USO assignment came through and he wanted to get overseas more than anything else. Anyway, he thought it would make bigger news later when he got back and had a chance to hunt every item down."

"Yes? Go on."

"That's all. That's all I know. What happened over there when he ran into Seabright is anybody's guess. He wrote me three letters with references to Seabright in them—not mentioning his name, of course—because of the censors. I could tell who he was referring to. The letters mean nothing unless one knows the whole story."

Suddenly there was a loud roll of the drums and the lights dimmed to a black-out. She reached into her handbag and took out a long brown envelope and handed it to me. "Here are the letters," she said.

I slipped the envelope into my breast pocket.

"Up until now," she went on, "I've considered all this my own business and none of your affair in spite of your threats. And none of that cheap R. E. Miller's affair either." Her tone was bitter. "But things have become so impossible for me that I'm forced to violate Harvey's confidence."

"I've been wondering why you chose to give this information to me instead of to Miller. Telling him would be the quickest way to call off the searching parties."

"That—that peacock!" She uttered a hysterical laugh. "Why, he thinks he's irresistible to women. He's going to learn a lesson for once in his life. Now"—she changed the subject abruptly—"now what do you do next? What are your plans?"

Before I had a chance to answer the floor show started right in front of our table and I decided to wait until it was over before continuing our conversation.

The entertainment was aggressively Russian to keep pace with the headlines. A girl wearing a red satin tunic sang a noisy and rousing Army song. She sounded all right most of the time, and the red satin took care of the times when she didn't. After the song she and two men in boots did a fierce dance full of stompings and whirls. Our table shook from the vibrations, and Mrs. Benson's cigarette case fell to the floor. She and I both bent down to pick it up. Her face was lighted by the glare of the spotlight. I was not voted the most popular boy in the class of '34, but ordinarily no one drummed up a revulsion for me after only two meetings. The dislike on her face was shocking. Apparently I had interfered too much with the comfort of Number One:

The next act was the headliner—a dagger dance in full Cossack regalia. The dancer was equipped with nine knives, three in each hand and three in his mouth. His movements were sure and graceful, but when he took to flipping the daggers from his mouth into a floor pad at our feet I wished we were sitting farther back. He did a great many tricks, spinning like a dervish all the while, and climaxed the act by pinning a ten-dollar bill to the pad with the nine knives. The spectators were enthusiastic—except for one drunk across the floor who kept up a boisterous commentary. "Aw, that's nothin'!" he shouted. "There's nothin' to it. Aw, I kin do it with my eyes closed. Come on, let an expert have a try at it, bud!"

The dancer, who appeared a humorless fellow to begin with, looked grim. I remember thinking that the drunk had better mind his own business or he'd get pinned to the mat himself. Meanwhile the dancer was repeating the trick with beautiful precision. The diners applauded. The drunk kept on scoffing.

Finally the dancer clapped his hands with decision. "All right, mister," he panted, "I tell you what. You come here. I give you one dagger. You pin the ten-dollar bill with only one dagger, the ten dollar yours."

A straw-haired chunky fellow pushed through the dark room onto the floor. He seemed familiar; possibly, I thought, because he looked like the prototype of all the rowdies whom liquor makes exhibitionistic—and then I remembered that he was the man who had come over from the Mayflower along with us.

He took the shiny knife from the dancer and ran his finger along the edge. Then he whistled. The crowd laughed. The music began softly. Suddenly I yelled and with all my strength dived across the table at Mrs. Benson, overturning her chair and landing beside her on the floor.

There was a huge commotion. The lights went up and I saw I had been too late. Winifred Benson lay staring up at me, but all the dislike had fled from her face. Her expression was startled, as if she'd been rudely interrupted while drawing a breath—as indeed she had been—for the dagger was standing upright in the soft flesh of her breast, and even as I watched a red trickle wound its way along the folds of her blue dress. The crowd pushed into a narrow black circle around me, and someone leaned over with a stiff shot of whisky, but Winifred Benson wouldn't ever be thirsty again. I drank it myself and stood up. The dagger dancer grabbed my arm and became elaborately hysterical in his own language. The headwaiter informed me some-one was calling the police, and then there was a gasping silence in the room as we all discovered that the drunk had vanished. There wasn't a trace of him, not even a bill to pay for the dinner that had turned cold upon his table.

16

The brightness beyond my eyelids must be the morning, I thought, but I didn't want to wake up. I wanted to stay in my dream with that sullen face beneath the straw-colored hair. I strained to recall if I had seen it before it appeared in the lobby of the Mayflower—in what building, in what room, on what street? But the circumstances lurked in a fog within my brain. If I could just tear away the mist, I thought, if I could just remember . . .

I was still trying to remember at eleven in the morning while Steve and I walked down the corridor of the Detective Bureau to Lieutenant Kaplan's office. In my vision the face seemed to have sunlight on it; I could distinguish every pore—but where, where had it been?

"Dad," Steve was saying, "Dad, why did that man at the desk wear a policeman's suit, Dad? Why did he?"

"He is a policeman."

"Well, what are you going to do in here, Dad? What are you—"

"I have to see a man about something, Steve."

"Do you have to see a policeman?"

"A kind of policeman." The face was there so near to mine, and in it the little green eyes were squinting . . .

"What kind of a policeman, Dad? What kind of a policeman—"

We came to a bench in the hall outside Lieutenant Kaplan's office. "You sit down here and wait for me, Steve," I said.

"Can't I come with you, Dad? Why can't I come with you? What are you going to do in there?"

There was a crooked stream of sweat crawling down the side of that face, and I was about to remember where . . .

"Dad, why can't I go in there with you, Dad?"

"Now you just sit down," I snapped at Steve. "Just sit down and be quiet for ten minutes, will you?"

When I had my hand on the doorknob I looked back. He was sitting on the bench, his shoulders drooping, his feet in scuffed saddle shoes hanging limply above the floor. His eyes, clouded with reproach, met mine. I unstrapped my wrist watch and walked over to him. "Steve," I said, "you can check on me. For every minute over ten that I'm in there I'll pay you a dime. O.K.? It's like a game, isn't it?"

I looked down at the silky spikes of his hair as he bent over the watch, his small pink lips unforgivingly tight together, and I thought how senselessly impatient I had been with him a moment before, how sharp my voice had been. Oh God, I thought, this Benson thing is getting me, working on my nerves. I can't even be relaxed with my own kid. And then I thought of the letters in my pocket that said so much while Winifred Benson was alive and so little now that she was dead. It seemed I no sooner laid my hands on a clue than it was snatched from me. I wasn't any farther along now than I had been a couple of weeks ago, and everything I needed had slipped through my hands. "Do you think anything makes any difference to a corpse?" Winifred Benson had asked. Maybe she was right. Maybe it would be best to give the whole thing up. I can have a perfectly clear conscience, I assured myself. I've done everything; I've tried everything. No one could blame me for giving up.

And I hadn't been so lighthearted in weeks as I was the minute after, when I walked into Lieutenant Kaplan's office and took the chair he offered me. He tossed a package of cigarettes across his desk.

"Have any bad dreams last night?" He grinned and pulled open a drawer. "I wouldn't blame you if you woke up screaming." He took out the dagger and ran his thumb appreciatively around its point and along its edge. "A wicked thing, a very wicked thing, eh? That Russian dancer is a strange cuss. Says he's been tossing these things around all over the world and was never insulted like that before." The lieutenant shook his head and drew a sheet of paper toward himself. "Except for the Barnum and Bailey trimmings, this would be a fairly routine manslaughter—but a couple of things are bothering us. In the first place, we haven't been able to find a trace of that drunk yet. In the second place, the waiter who took care of him reports he didn't order any drinks. That doesn't mean too much. The guy might have been drunk when he got there, but the waiter says not, says he acted perfectly all right until the knife trouble started. I know we heard your version last night, but since you've slept on it can you enlighten us any more?"

"You know, I'm sure I've seen that guy somewhere before I saw him in the Mayflower. He's connected in my mind with some sort of disagreeable experience, but I can't recall." I rubbed my forehead. "I've had so much on my mind lately—"

The lieutenant nodded. "Sure. I know, the harder you try to remember, the further it gets from you. It'll come. Let's talk about this poor woman"—he consulted his notes—"Winifred Benson. Was she a friend of yours?"

"I met her for the first time just a week ago. She's the widow of an old friend, Harvey Benson, the radio commentator."

"Yeah—I remember him."

"She knew I was living here, and when she got to town she called me up. The Mayflower was jammed, so we went around the corner to the Volga Room, worse luck."

The telephone on the desk buzzed and the lieutenant spoke into it about fingerprinting someone, and then I heard him say, "The jewelry store on the corner. It looked like an inside job and—"

My sharp exclamation startled him. "I've got it," I whispered. He nodded, spoke a few more words into the telephone, and hung up.

I began to explain. "It was at one of the street interviews I was doing for the Logan Company. This guy spouted some anti-minority stuff into the mike, and when I tried to stop him he got rough." I told the lieutenant of our scuffle and my assailant's subsequent humiliation at the hands of the marine.

"Sounds like he's an all-round bad actor," the lieutenant commented. "Say, do you suppose that knife was meant for you?"

"Why should he try to kill me over a little brawl like I that?"

"Can't tell about those birds. Might have wanted to hurt you a little. Can't remember his name, can you?"

I shook my head.

The lieutenant made some more notes. "Well, we've a good description of him," he told me, "and we'll do our damnedest to pick him up. When we do I'll want you to come in again." He said he'd call when there was anything new to report. We shook hands and I left.

Steve leaped up from the bench. "You owe me fourteen dimes!" he shouted.

"Wow!" I took out my wallet and paid him. "Five minutes more and you'd have to buy our lunch."

"Do you know what, Dad?" He took my hand and we walked down the hall. "I like the food much better here than at home."

Apprehensively I recalled the week's menus. "If you come to Washington to live," I made my voice stern—"we can't go on skipping vegetables the way we have been."

"I know it."

"Now, since it's your last day, you choose where we'll go for lunch."

"The zoo."

"Steve, you know they don't serve anything there but hot dogs and ice cream."

"Well, I'm not living down here yet," he pointed out with airy patience. "I'm only visiting."

When we got home Frances Rhodes was bug-eyed with obvious admiration for a well-tailored white-haired gentleman sitting in the lobby's single chair. It was Carlos San Martin. He rose when he saw us.

"Good afternoon, good afternoon," he said, bowing deeply, "and this is the junior Mr. Pike?"

"What brings you here, Mr. San Martin?" I asked him. "Were you waiting to see me?"

He nodded, his eyes on Steve. "If possible, privately, most privately."

I asked Steven to play outdoors for a few minutes, and Carlos and I went upstairs. I couldn't think of any reason why he should want to see me alone, but all the same his presence threw a cloud over my day. Now what's coming? I wondered, and I felt the same discomfort I had on the dark terrace that first night of our meeting.

"Would you like a drink?" I asked him when we were in the apartment. "I'd like one myself. I'm more or less celebrating today."

He made a gesture of agreement with his soft small hand. When I had poured the whisky he said, "This is an anniversary of some significance, no? Then perhaps the beginning of some auspicious venture?"

"Both wrong." I raised my glass. "To the ending of a most inauspicious adventure."

"Ah? Then it is appropriate that we drink together to-day, you know. I, too, have come to an ending. I have decided to leave the United States and return to my own country. I feel there is fine opportunity for me there now that the war is over."

"Well," I said, "well well."

"From here to my country is a very long trip, Mr. Pike."

"Yes, it is, isn't it?"

"And a very expensive trip. Also, I shall need a little cash for investment, for living expenses, et cetera. With-out cash I shall be quite handicapped, you know."

I waited.

"Ah? And I have so little cash. The war, the high cost of living—everything has been very bad for me the past years." He crossed his legs, and I saw his elegant silk-clad ankle and his small glossy black shoe. "Now, Mr. Pike, I have thought of a way to get the money I will be needing and also, at the same time, to do you a great favor."

"How have you figured that out?"

"I have something to sell. Something you want to buy. If we can arrange a transaction we shall each be the hap-piest of men."

"What are you talking about? What kind of transac-tion?"

He drew out an initialed alligator wallet, removed a newspaper clipping, and handed it to me. It was from the *Post* of that morning—I had read it over breakfast—an account of the circumstances surrounding the death of Winifred Benson in the Volga Room the night before. My name and my account of the incident were mentioned at the end of the article.

"Terrible thing that this woman died, is it not, Mr. Pike?" Carlos was saying. "She'd have made a very good and necessary corroboration of your suspicions as to who killed Harvey Benson. Now you are at a great disadvantage, I imagine; now you are wondering what to do next?" He stared at me with beaming beady eyes. "Suppose I were to tell you what to do next? Suppose I were to get you absolute proof—eyewitness proof—"

I clutched my glass until my knuckles ached. "What do you know about it?"

Carlos's lips opened in a wide grin over the two far-apart front teeth. "I know all about it," he said softly. "That is the information I will sell you, my dear Mr. Pike, for fifteen thousand dollars."

"You can go to hell."

He shrugged and took a long drink. "I wish to make you a very fair proposition. You put the fifteen thousand on a table. I tell you my story, bring you my proofs. If you are not satisfied, if you do not feel it is your money's worth, you pick up the fifteen thousand and put it in your pocket. Good-by. If you are satisfied, I pick it up. That is fair, is it not?"

"Mr. San Martin, what makes you think that even if I were curious about Benson's death I'd be willing to pay for information?"

"You are of a certain tenacity of temperament. I recognize it."

"Then perhaps I ought to tell you that what I'm celebrating today is the end of my interest in the Benson matter. You're too late, Mr. San Martin. I'm giving up the whole thing."

"Truly? Do you promise? For in that case I cancel my intention for leaving the country. I shall carry out my original plan after all." He sighed lengthily. "I shall have to indulge in blackmail."

"Of whom?"

"Ah-ah." He shook his finger playfully. "That costs money."

"From what I hear, there's usually more than fifteen thousand in blackmail."

"But it's dangerous," he reproached me. "I, too, am apt to be in automobile accidents, to be the target of knives—"

"The knife—what happened last night—had nothing to do with Benson."

"Maybe yes. Maybe no. However, I should much prefer dealing with you."

"You're wasting your time. I wouldn't pay for information even if I had the money, and I haven't a cent."

"My dear Mr. Pike, I knew as much. I count on your borrowing it."

"Where?"

"But from Martha, certainly. But of course. Now I know what you're going to say. Why would she give it to you? Because, my dear Mr. Pike, she loves you." He hunched his shoulders and spread his hands in that typically Latin gesture of "That's life." "I have known her for many months and watched her with many men, and take my word for it, she loves you."

I stood up and went to the window and stared out of it onto the thick green treetops below. There was a small playground across the street, and I watched Steve's small blue-clad figure go ceaselessly down the slide, up the ladder and down the slide again. She loves me, I repeated to myself.

"Ah, Mr. Pike," came Carlos's soft, insidious voice behind me. "Martha Finchley is a beautiful woman, a magnetic woman. I have wanted her. Then you came along hardly a month ago and presto I realize I have no chance.

So I retreat to an old plan of mine. Get some money and return to my native land. Understand? That brings us to this moment." I turned around and sat down. He moved uneasily in his chair. There was a quarter inch of melted ice in the bottom of his glass. He drank it. He crossed his legs again. Finally he said. "That brings us to the transaction I mentioned before."

"Mr. San Martin," I said, "there can be no transaction between us. Forget about extortion, will you, and bring your friend here. Do it as—as a good deed."

"A good deed in such a naughty world, as the great poet put it?" He uncovered his whole set of white teeth and shook his head. "Really, I have no time to hold up little candles in the darkness. I am quite helpless. I need the money." He stood up and took his hat. "I'll give you time to think it over."

"Time won't change anything. I told you before, I'm dropping my interest in the Benson matter. I'm through."

"Well, too bad, too bad. So many changes of plans." He wagged his head back and forth. "Senator Witherell too. I understand he has been quite unwell and has decided to announce his resignation next week." He raised his hand at my stare of surprise. "Better think it over, Mr. Pike. I have patience. You call me in a day or two?"

When he had left I went back to the window and watched Steve, who by this time had dispensed with the ladder and was climbing back up the slide on all fours. A moment later I saw the top of Carlos's dapper gray hat as he left the apartment and walked busily up the street. Steve began to belly-slam down the slide. He had on his last clean suit, but I didn't make any move to call him or stop him. I wanted to be up there alone for a while and think about things.

17

Early the next morning I put Steve on a Cleveland plane. A fresh-skinned stewardess with very good teeth and legs patted his head, and squeezed his hand, said she was sure they'd have a beautiful flight. I said I was sure they would too. Steve wanted to know what would happen if there should be thunder and lightning. There wouldn't be, I told him. It was a fine clear day. Well, what if his grandfather wasn't at the airport when he got to Cleveland? But he absolutely would be, I said. Well, he said, what if the pilot steered the plane too low and they bumped into the Washington Monument? The stewardess laughed. The pilot was an ace fighter during the war. The pilot wouldn't do anything that silly. When it was time for me to leave Steve clung to my hand.

"When am I coming to live with you?"

"Very soon."

"How soon?"

"Maybe by Christmas."

"Promise by Christmas?" He tugged at my fingers. "Promise?"

"All right."

He settled back in his seat while I buckled the safety belt. "I'll tell everyone to send my presents down here," he said.

I bent over him. "Good-by, Steve, I'll be seeing you."

Suddenly he threw his arms about my neck and I felt his soft small mouth push into my cheek, and he was kissing me for the first time.

"My, he likes his daddy, doesn't he?" said the stewardess.

I waited on the field until the plane took off and until it was just a precious bright silver speck dissolving northward in the sky. Then I ate breakfast in the airport coffee shop, read the *Post,* walked around to the telephones to call Martha, changed my mind about that, wandered back through the waiting room, and passed a magazine stand. There were a dozen copies of a popular weekly clipped to a wire over the stand, and a dozen big photographs of that handsome, blond, strong-jawed, all-American face stared out of them, presumably at the man with a vote. In black type at the bottom of the cover were the words: "Lloyd M. Seabright, An Intimate Portrait of a Valuable American, by Howard Linzell."

One look at those twelve blatant covers pulled a switch in my head. All the gears and belts and wheels that had been going full force since Carlos had made his proposition froze into silence, and the plan they had been drowning out sounded clear as a starter's whistle.

A half-hour later I walked down a long corridor of the Senate Office Building until I came to the right door and opened it and walked in. There was a young woman sitting at a desk opening the mail, the white fluffy collar on her dark dress still fresh as the morning. The carpet and the walls in the room were green, and several green filing cabinets stood along one wall. The nine o'clock sunlight spilled through the Venetian blinds and flashed off the silver letter opener in the secretary's hand. As I stood there her neat pink-tipped hands stopped their movements.

"I'd like to see the senator," I said, "if he's in."

"Do you have an appointment?"

"No, but the senator knows me. My name is Alexander Pike."

"Oh yes!" Her voice put the words into italics.

"I'll see," she said, and went into the next office. I told myself it was a good omen that the old boy got down early, a sign that I was having some luck for a change.

The secretary opened the door and beckoned to me. When I passed her she said, "You haven't a microphone in your pocket, have you, Mr. Pike?"

I remember her saying that because after I'd been in there with the senator for a while I was wishing I had a mike and that someone else had been listening to that incredible dialogue with me.

If the outer office looked like sunshine and morning, the senator's private office was night and mourning. A stage designer couldn't have put the feeling across any more decisively. It was in the blinds drawn against the light, in the somber massive furniture, in the relic-of-a-past-age marble fireplace, in the fragile figure of the man who stood to greet me, and in the fleshless, dry touch of his hand. I had watched the senator from the gallery many times and I had seen him close up twice in the rosy, ex-hilarated atmosphere of Martha's home, but he had never looked like this. Carlos had said he was sick. This man holding a cigarette box out in his shaking fingers, leaning his brittle pale skull against the leather chair back, this man was almost dead.

"Sit down, Mr. Pike, sit down." Miraculously his voice was unchanged, still deep, sonorous, compelling. I thought of all the times it had sounded in the Congress, in the newsreels, over the radio, in the assembly halls of America and Europe. "It's good of you to call on me." His light eyes peered at me from behind his glasses. "Things have been going well with the show, I hope? From all the reports, I hear you've got a winner. I suppose"—he smiled and the skin of his face crinkled like tissue paper—"it's a bit early to tell."

"I'm pretty confident, sir," I told him. "I think it's going to be a big and long-lived success."

"You won't mind that?"

"I don't think I'll be staying with the show, Senator."

"What's the trouble, Mr. Pike?"

"Well, that's what I've come to see you about. It's—"

"Oh, but, I'm sure—" His eyes stared vaguely past me. "I'm afraid—I don't think there's anything I can do—"

"I didn't come to ask you to save my job. I came to ask you not to resign from the Senate. Not yet. I came to ask you to wait."

He reached up and took off his glasses, and now his light eyes were on mine.

"Go on, Mr. Pike. Explain yourself, please."

"The rumor about town is that you're going to resign next week. I hope it's not true."

"I am waiting for you to explain, Mr. Pike."

"Will you give me several minutes, sir? It's a complicated story. It's about Lloyd Seabright."

His thin speckled hand pressed a button, and the secretary opened the door.

"I don't want to be disturbed until I ring," the senator told her.

The door clicked shut, and there I was facing the old man and ready to tell again the tale I had told so often in the past few days. Steve's voice sounded distantly inside my head—*Promise by Christmas*—and I lighted a fresh cigarette, waiting for it to shut up. Then I started to talk— beginning where it had all begun, the day of the Victory Parade, when Hal Corbett told me Benson had drowned himself.

When I was through the senator seemed hardly to notice that I had ceased speaking. For almost a full minute he stared straight ahead. Then he got up from his desk and walked across the room. He moved like Father Time himself, as if bowed beneath the weight of an invisible scythe, until he reached the fireplace. The summer's pleated paper fan still hid its opening. The senator leaned against the marble mantel.

"Mr. Pike, you haven't got a case. I was a lawyer before I was a senator. You haven't got a case."

"Give me time. Give me a few weeks and I'll come to you with a clear case."

"Are you trying to tell me you're going to prove Lloyd Seabright killed a man? Is that what you have in mind? Are you trying to tell me he killed Benson?"

"I don't know. I know he tried to kill me. Listen, sir, even if Lloyd Seabright never killed a fly, he isn't fit to be a United States senator. He isn't fit to take your place, sit in your seat, be your successor, endorsed by you. Maybe I haven't got a case yet—but what about the story San Martin offered to sell me?"

"What's the story?"

"I haven't fifteen thousand dollars to pay for it."

"Neither have I." The old man gestured with an empty hand and let it fall to his side. "Buying information about people is a kind of monkey business I don't indulge in. Besides, that San Martin impresses me as a slick character—"

"All right, leave him out of it. But what about everything I've told you? What about the threads that weave and interweave? Look, Senator, Seabright was in Italy when Benson was. Seabright's future secretary went to Fucino with Benson. Seabright's secretary lied to me about the circumstances of Benson's death—"

"How can you be sure?"

"It was obvious, I tell you. Then she disappears. Why else would she leave town except to avoid further questioning? Then a law firm in Chicago sends one of its operators to Mrs. Benson to recover a mysterious story. The senior partner in this same firm is known to be a supporter and pivot financial man for undercover fascist organizations. The senior partner in this firm represents Seabright. I start digging into it and Seabright tries to kill me. Now can't you infer that—"

"Mr. Pike, I am too tired to infer anything about anything. You haven't got a case."

"Then you're not going to do anything?"

He turned his head and looked at the oil painting above the fireplace. It was a portrait of himself twenty or thirty years younger, the skin still tight, the blue eyes vivid, the hair thick and graying. It was the portrait that would someday be used in the history books.

"If I were that man, I might," he said. He shuffled back to his desk and sat down again in the polished leather chair.

"You see I am a sick old man, Mr. Pike. A very tired old man. I am not fit to be in the Senate either—"

"But, sir, I—"

"Wait, I want you to hear this. It has been my own shameful secret for a long time. Now I want to talk about it. Mr. Pike, my usefulness was finished a half-dozen years ago. I should have quit then. I knew my mind was dulling. I'd lose track in discussions; I'd fall asleep in committees. Too old, Mr. Pike, too old. I was trying to ignore my blood and my nerves and my heart." The network of wrinkles on his face deepened. "Once in a while a man can outlast a seventy-five-year-old body. In here"—he tapped his forehead—"once in a while the vigor is still left, the vigor and the manhood. Mine was gone six years ago. I recall the very moment I knew.

"I was debating on the floor with a junior senator from a Western state. While I was talking I saw him looking at me, this young man separated from me by four decades, by more than a generation. It was the expression on his face— as if all my mirrors had been misty and his face was my first clear mirror. Your life is over, old man, his face said; we're talking about a day when all you'll have of this country will be six feet of earth. It's our lives, our country, our future now. All he said out loud was, 'I don't believe you heard me correctly, Senator.' That was the moment I knew."

"But you ran for re-election?"

He shrugged. His eyes moved again to that distant point beyond my shoulder. "I had to. I was broke. I had a household, obligations, and no income. What could I do in the outside world at my age? I've served most of my life in the Congress, but there is no pension for men like me. What could I do? But last year my wife passed away"—his voice quavered—"and I'm sick and I'm getting out if I have to live in a tent. I'm getting out!"

"Couldn't you at least get the governor to appoint someone else instead of Seabright?"

"Impossible. All the machinery is in motion now for me to announce my resignation next Monday, and I'm not going to change it. What reason can I give the governor? I've already agreed to the appointment of Seabright."

"Next Monday! Then all I've told you means nothing?"

"Seabright is a capable man, in his prime, of good reputation. Extremely intelligent. You have proof of that on your radio show, haven't you? Now, Mr. Pike, you are too hard. A man who has made a mistake in the past may still turn out to be a fine, useful, and brilliant public servant."

"Is murder a mistake, Senator? Is supporting hatemongering, malicious anti-American organizations a mistake?" I stood up. "When a patriot no longer cares about those things, he is old," I said angrily. "Too damn old."

He didn't answer me.

"Then it's final that you won't do anything?" I demanded.

He moved his head slightly from side to side.

In silence I walked to the door and left.

It was like leaving a tomb. Outside I was surprised to find the sun still shining and that it was only ten o'clock in the morning of one of those soft and beautiful days that come to Washington in the autumn. I went home, read my mail, answered a few telephone calls, and wondered what to do next. The script of next Sunday's show lay on the table. I picked it up and went over it again. Our guests were to be an ambassador, a very old and famous admiral, a female correspondent just back from China, a congressman from the Northwest. The suggested cues and conversational gambits were written in just as Martha and I had agreed on them. As in the previous show, the topics we chose covered a lot of ground, since the special interests of our guests were so varied. Since the Ambassador was from a small oriental country whose history was both exotic and obscure, we had penciled in several questions to ask him. That would be one subject at least on which Lloyd would have little to say, I reflected. And then another, much bigger, more important, thought struck me and I scowled at the paper, not seeing the words, just letting a question roll around in my mind, waiting for it to be snagged on something and answered.

The question was: How does it happen that Lloyd is so thoroughly well informed on every single topic that came up on the show? Was it only coincidence? Was he really that brilliant? Did he have one of those memories that fasten onto everything ever heard or read? Or was there another reason? I sat in the chair thinking about that until the telephone rang about a quarter hour later.

"Hello, hello," I snarled.

"Hello," Martha said.

"What the hell do you want?"

"I just wanted to hear if you were all right."

"Why shouldn't I be?"

"The Volga Room seems to be a dangerous place."

When I didn't answer she went on, "I—I read about what happened. It was a dreadful thing."

"Yes, it was."

"I'm sorry. I know how you must feel. That must be a horrible thing to have happen to you."

"It happened to Mrs. Benson, not me. I'm sorry I can't tell her you're sorry."

"Darling, I know you've a right to be mad at me for the way I banged out the other night. How about a reconciliation scene on horseback?"

"What?"

"Let's go riding. It's such a wonderful day. Remember, once you said that we'd have to—"

"I remember everything I said and everything you said."

"Doesn't it crowd your mind terribly? You must need some fresh air and exercise. Besides, we can talk."

"Since when is that an inducement to you?"

"Come on, darling, I've apologized about the other night. Call up that place you go to and arrange it, will you?"

"I don't know if I can get any horses," I said crossly, "and besides, it's going to rain. The witch is out."

"She's crazy. Pick me up as soon as you've changed. All right?"

"All right."

She rang off and I told Frances to get me Charlie Thurston's stables.

18

In Rock Creek Park the sun was gentle on our heads and on the smooth flanks of our horses. We cantered up- and downhill, through the bright fallen leaves on the paths, and once as we drew near the Maryland line a red fox faced us on the trail, then turned and bounded into the brush. Finally we stopped exchanging impersonal comments about the weather, the scenery, the riders who passed us, and walked our horses side by side in silence.

After a while Martha said, "It seems that the chitchat is over. Now we can get on with the talk. What have you got on your chest today, Alexander?"

"Is that the purpose of this ride? A sort of therapeutic measure to relieve the pressure on my chest?"

"The ride is because it's such a wonderful day and because I want to be with you on it."

I looked at her clear, perfectly modeled profile under the brown felt hat, at her slender shoulders in the tweed coat. I admired how knowing and light her hands were on the reins, how expertly she sat.

"Martha," I said, "there are a lot of things I can't figure out, and the knottiest one is you. Why are you tied up with Lloyd—promoting Lloyd, engrossed in Lloyd's career? What's it all about? Why do you do it? Why?"

"Heavens," she said, "the inquiring reporter!" She smiled, but her eyes were serious under the soft slanting brim of her hat. "You know, the first time I met Lloyd it was here, riding in the park. Years and years ago. We both kept our horses at the Fieldstone Club and used to nod to each other going in and out. Then one day he talked to me. I'd been married and living in Washington for a long time, but it might as well have been Washington State for all I saw of Capital society. I felt lonely and snubbed. Lloyd changed all that. He introduced me to people that, left to myself, I'd never have met. After all—who was I? Just a totally unheard-of girl from the sticks. As for my husband— Oscar was a lot older and set in his ways and wrapped up in his business. He liked to be sociable, but he didn't care with whom. People were just people. I'd never have gotten out of that paralyzing dullness, away from his friends, if I'd had to count on him. It was Lloyd who plugged me and stood by me during all the rebuffs I had to take, during all the times I had to be so embarrassingly pushing and aggressive. Let me tell you, darling, it wasn't easy. I developed a shell like a turtle's or I would have committed suicide. But I got what I wanted and Lloyd helped me. Now I'd like to help him get what he wants. Simple, isn't it?"

"Then it's a matter of obligation on your part?"

She leaned forward and stroked the neck of her mount. "Not entirely. I'm very fond of Lloyd. He's my alter ego. Wherever he goes, I, in a manner of speaking, go too. Whatever he becomes, I become. Whatever I can't do because of what and who I am—he can do and I share in it. We're each others creations, and I'm proud of him."

"You approve of all his machinations? Such as his financial support of the most virulent, malicious, screwball organization in this country—the American Challengers?"

Her cheeks spotted red with anger. "That's a lie. Who told you that?"

"Mrs. Benson."

"She lied. She deserved to be struck dead. That's a lie."

"So the way you look at it is that Lloyd's avenging guardian angel strikes down everyone who wants to expose him? I didn't know you were so superstitious. At any rate, Lloyd's involvement with the Challengers was the story Benson intended to give out. At least that's the way I analyze it."

The trail narrowed and we came to a steep bank over the creek where the earth sheered away into a thirty-foot drop to the shallow rushing stream below. Martha prodded her horse ahead of mine, and for a few minutes we rode single file without speaking. When we were again abreast Martha said:

"The whole thing is too preposterous to argue about. I know Lloyd and, unless I'm completely blind and stupid, these things you say can't be true."

"Why are you so sure? You know how politically ambitions he is."

"But it would be self-defeating. A good reputation, a clean record, is worth a million times more than any dirty business with such people." She made a grimace of disapproval. "I've seen the type. I sat near some of the Challengers in the Senate gallery during a debate before the war. The looks of their faces were frightening—and pathetic too. One of them was right in front of me. I kept thinking, That is a man who wants hate to split us up. That man in the wilted jacket and dirty-edged collar, that man with the dandruff flaking through his hair! How far did they get? Did you ever hear a peep out of the Challengers during the war?"

"The war is over and unfortunately dandruff isn't a fatal disease. They're back and they're growing. They might just be able to swing some elections one of these days."

"But not for Lloyd. Lloyd would have everything to lose!"

"Maybe he doesn't figure that way. Maybe there's a part of him that's totally unexplored country to you—"

She shook her head impatiently. "For some reason you've gone haywire because of your dislike for him. You'd be a lot happier if you didn't go about trying to analyze everything and everybody."

"Perhaps you're right. Analyzing doesn't get me anywhere near as far as cash might. Carlos San Martin called on me yesterday, by the way."

"What did he want?"

"Fifteen thousand dollars. He says that would cover the cost of the information I need to clinch my case against Lloyd."

"What information? How does he know anything about it? It must be a joke!" When I didn't answer she demanded again, "Is it a joke?"

"Without the money I'll never know."

"But what's going on? How could he know anything about Lloyd?" she insisted. "Why, he's just a—a high-class junk dealer."

"He gets around, doesn't he?"

"Sure he gets around. The way a gigolo gets around. Because of his face and his manners and because he's a male animal." Her voice was scornful. "Nothing boosts popularity quicker around this town than the right pants and the right to wear them."

"Is that the case on S Street too?"

"Certainly. That and his persistence. And besides, he's entertaining. But when it comes to playing he's a gumshoe, and selling mysterious information— Oh, he's carrying things much too far."

"He suggested I get the money from you."

She threw back her head and laughed merrily.

"Now really! Can't you see it's a gag? Oh, I'll have to scold him for this nonsense."

"Since I expected your reaction would be what it is, I went to Senator Witherell this morning. Don't worry," I answered her glare of fury, "it didn't do any good. He's senile. He wouldn't believe me either."

She tightened her lips. "You've been a very, very busy boy, haven't you, darling? And what other mischief were you up to early this morning? I called and couldn't get an answer."

"I had to put Steve on the plane."

"Oh—so he's gone. When will he come again?"

"I said something about Christmas just to keep him happy—but I won't be here then, of course. If my luck continues this way I'll probably be knocking around New York unemployed."

"What do you mean, Alec? What about the show?"

"I'm quitting after this Sunday. I'm sorry to give you so little notice, but I just made up my mind this morning."

"Alec! How can you do that just when—"

"I can't stay and agree to the fast work you're pulling, Martha. I suddenly realized that you're coaching Lloyd—that he sees the script ahead of time. We're passing off the show as spontaneous and unrehearsed, and you know it isn't—you're cheating. Just in the two times we've been on the air Lloyd's peculiar brilliance on every subject that comes up has attracted attention. I know it's all part of the promotional plan to make Lloyd's appointment look good. Now that Witherell is resigning so suddenly Lloyd will get the appointment, anyway, and all your bother was really unnecessary."

She didn't deny any of it. She merely said, "You're leaving after Sunday night?"

"Yes. And one more thing. I'm going to throw out the script we planned and do a new one by myself. I'd rather

not play the poor sap even once more, if you don't mind."
I heard the little sound she made as she drew in her breath.
She turned to me, her eyes narrowed and black with anger.

"I don't mind if you quit right now, you great big plaster saint! You're fired!"

She gave her horse a sharp kick and galloped off down the path, and the suggestive mare I was riding rushed like hell after her. It was quite a race through the woods, beside the creek, up again onto the high banks. Under other circumstances I would have enjoyed it. Finally the trail ended at a road, and across it in a small clearing I saw Martha talking to a man on a beautiful chestnut hunter. I reined in my horse and walked toward them, and suddenly excitement stabbed at my heart. The man was Lloyd Seabright. Martha must have arrived only a moment before me, for the flanks of her horse still heaved between her legs. I didn't think she had had time to tell Lloyd about our conversation. I wondered if the senator had phoned him after I left. I wondered how he was going to act.

He acted precisely as usual. Greeted me with a smile and held out his hand. He offered us both cigarettes and lit one for himself, and we engaged in our customary beating-about-the-bush conversation, pretending by tacit agreement that things were just what they seemed. Martha paid no attention to me.

"I didn't dream I'd find you out today," Lloyd said to her. "I saw Shane in his stall when I went out."

"I rented the horses," I said, "from Charlie Thurston."

"Who's he?"

"He has a stable near Oak Street off Sixteenth Street."

"You'd better be hurrying back there. It's going to storm."

Martha and I both looked skyward. For the first time I noticed that the day had turned dark; the sun was blotted out by heavy fast-moving clouds. The Weather Wizard had been right.

"Well, that's a surprise!" Martha said.

"We're going to get caught," I predicted.

"Come on," Lloyd announced with abrupt determination. "I'll show you the shortest way back. I know the trails blindfolded."

"But what about you?" I asked.

"Fieldstone's just over there." He gestured behind him, and through the trees I saw a stable and part of a fenced-in ring. "I can get you started and get back in time."

Martha shook her head. "Don't bother, Lloyd. A little rain won't hurt us."

"It's going to be a big rain. Come this way. I'll show you."

She held up her hand in a short gesture of farewell and put her horse into a fast canter across the road and back up the way we had come.

"Go down the other way," Lloyd shouted to me. He brought his crop down hard on the rump of my mare, and she started along a path on our side of the road. Lloyd was coming along fast behind me. He struck at the mare again. "We'll show her!" he called. "We'll show her!"

I remember that just then I heard a distant ominous roll of thunder, and the nearer thunder of the hunter's hoofs. My mare, exhilarated by this new chase, rushed wildly on. I remember dodging the low branches which hung over the trail and how the mare leaped and strained to keep ahead of the racing hunter, and I knew I'd never stop her until she wanted to be stopped. Fury swelled in me at Lloyd for having started this thing and turned into horror when the great body beneath me stumbled and pitched forward and then, as I lifted the reins, luckily recovered.

The rest comes back to me in a nightmarish jumble. I know there was more thunder and that lightning flashed among the trees and that suddenly I noticed the ground fell away to my right and we were high above the creek. A voice inside me said that drop would be murder, and as I tightened the left rein I can recall how the mare's head turned and her left eye rolled wildly and I felt her rear into the air. I heard myself scream—a short, piercing, hideous sound—and next, miraculously, it was the trail, not the creek, that hurtled up to meet me. I lay there breathless in the dirt and leaves, listening to the mare rolling and crashing down the bank into the rocky water below.

"Alec," Martha said, "Alec, Alec, Alec."

I opened my eyes.

"Oh, Alec darling," she said, and she put her head down on my chest and sobbed.

"Ouch," I said.

She lifted her head immediately. "Did that hurt you, darling? Where do you hurt? Do you think anything's broken?" I noticed that she had lost her hat, and her hair had come loose and straggled about her smudged face.

"How did you get here?" I asked her.

"I changed my mind. I turned around and came this way to be with you. I was right behind Lloyd. I saw the whole thing." She took my hand into her own and held it to her cheek.

I wanted to lie there quietly with my fingers next to her soft flesh and her face so different, so tender above me. I knew that if I moved a hundred little agonies would careen up and down my body, but I moved anyway. I hoisted myself up on my elbows.

"Lloyd started that runaway," I told her. "That makes one more score I'll have to even up with him." I groaned and lay back on the ground. "Jesus, that was close—awfully close." I shuddered, and across my mind there flashed the vision of a girl in a black dirndl who had waved to me one morning when we marched up the streets of a French town. We had gone through a lot of heavy bombardment just the day before, and when I saw this girl's face and her white arm waving a little flag in the sunshine a great wave of nausea rolled over me at the thought of death. She was not even a pretty girl, but suddenly not to have seen her face, not the hair flying back from a point on her forehead, not the perspiration shining along her lip, or the little white picket teeth she flashed at me—suddenly that was the most horrible deprivation I could think of, and as we tramped up the dusty street I felt the first deep tearing fear I had known since I'd been in action. I mustn't die, I kept telling myself, I mustn't die.

"Is—is the mare dead?" I asked Martha.

"From here she looks terribly dead."

"Oh God, I don't know what made that poor foolish animal rear!"

"I do."

"What was it? Something cockeyed about my horsemanship? They say the sporting thing to do after, a spill is to get right back in the saddle. I guess I'm not a sport. What happened?"

"I'll tell you about it when we get you home."

"Where's Lloyd?"

"He's gone to get his car. He'll drive down to the road and help me get you into it. Does anything feel broken, darling? I'll call a doctor as soon as—"

"You won't have to. I'm just bruised, I think. Now are you convinced I'm not made out of plaster after all?"

"You needn't have gone to so much trouble to convince me, darling."

Then it began to rain in earnest. Big steady sheets of it. Martha took off her coat and covered me.

"For an ex-boss you're being very considerate of an ex-employee," I said.

We stayed there smiling at each other and holding hands until Lloyd came.

Martha had insisted they take me to her home. Her butler half carried me upstairs and into a bedroom. He pulled off my wet things and piled blankets over me.

I heard Lloyd's voice and Martha's answering and then the sound of a door closing. A couple of minutes later she came in with a tray of glasses and a whisky bottle. She poured me a shot, which I willingly drank down.

"Thomas," she said to the butler, "take Mr. Pike's keys, go over to his apartment, and bring back a complete change of clothing."

When he had left she poured me another shot and one for herself. I heard the bottle tinkle against the glasses as if her hand were unsteady, and when she sat down on the bed beside me with the drink I saw she was trembling.

"Hey there," I said, "what's the matter?"

"I—I'll get over it. It's a—a kind of delayed reaction, I guess. Oh, Alec—" Her voice broke and she put her hand over her eyes.

"Thanks for letting it mean that much to you. Thanks very much, dear."

"You know this is the first time you've ever called me anything affectionate like that?"

"First time out loud, maybe."

And then because I felt my love for her was going to well up and burst out of my mouth in the form of some passionate declaration which I couldn't at the moment follow up, I looked desperately around for another subject.

"This is a beautiful room," I said.

"It's mine."

I glanced again at the pale green hangings, the mirrors, the little skyline of perfume bottles on the dressing table, and on the night stand next to my head a copy of *The Managerial Revolution.*

"Yes, it's like you."

Martha put her empty glass down on the tray with a decisive bang and stood up.

"I'm having some lunch brought up here," she said. "By the time you eat it I'll be back. I've got to go to the bank to get that fifteen thousand dollars."

"Martha!"

"Your horsemanship wasn't cockeyed." That new tender look was on her face as she bent over me. "Lloyd jammed his lighted cigarette into the mare's rump. I saw him." She kissed me and went out, closing the door behind her.

19

By the time Thomas came back with the station wagon and my clothes I had finished lunch. To the accompaniment of several fervent moans I got myself dressed. Then I looked up the number of Carlos's shop and called him. The telephone in the bedroom was a pale green color, but it worked all right. Carlos said he was delighted to hear from me. I told him that Martha and I would like to come over to see him within the next half-hour.

"You mean you want the information I mentioned yesterday?"

"That's right."

"And are you coming with the proper preparations?"

"You wouldn't reconsider and let sweet smiles and coaxing words be the proper preparations, would you, old boy?"

He chuckled. "I'm sorry, Mr. Pike. I am a victim of circumstances. Now I do not think it would be so good for you to come here to the shop. Interruptions. Customers. No, come to my house."

"What's the address?"

"I'm in Georgetown. Martha knows the location well, Mr. Pike," he said smugly. "I go right home now and wait for you."

When Martha arrived a few minutes later I told her about it.

"Let's be on our way." She patted the brown suede bag slung over her shoulder. "It's all here," she said.

"That's a lot of lettuce. Are you sure you want to—"

"It's a cheap way to protect your life, darling. Come on. I'll drive."

Georgetown is probably the only place below the Mason-Dixon line where white people yearn, sigh, and fight each other for houses next door to Negroes. The location is so ultra-desirable that there are long waiting lists for vacancies. Of course the remodeled houses occupied by whites are mansions compared with the crumbling Negro tenements next door to them—but just the same, the Negroes are next door, the little colored babies play on the curb, the adults lean in the doorways. It is one more cruel unanswerable riddle that in Georgetown this proximity is considered so valuable it hikes the rent, while in the movie houses, the theatres, the concert halls, it is strictly forbidden.

Carlos lived in the narrowest house I had ever seen. It was white painted brick, just one room wide and three stories high. In the second-floor window there were bright chintz curtains and a shining copper tureen of ivy. Behind it we saw his face peering briefly at us. A moment later the door opened.

"Come in. Come in. Welcome. My dear Martha." He kissed her hand.

"You know, Carlos," she said, removing her hand from under his face, "I never figured you'd do anything like this."

"But why? I walk into your department store. I want a sable coat for a friend. Do you instruct the clerk to give it to me? Do you say, 'Fine, you're welcome, wrap it up, take it away'?" His tone was aggrieved. "You know economics better than that, my dear lady."

He led us upstairs into the living room. I don't understand the fuss people make over used and worm-eaten old furniture, but if you have to have antiques I suppose his kind are the kind to have. Everything looked very fragile and expensive. All around the room there was a profusion of ivy growing out of unlikely-looking places such as drawers, inkstands, decanters, lamp bases, and what looked like an old penny bank.

He saw me looking at it. "Once upon a time that was an old penny bank!" he cried proudly.

I took it that any object which would function as an ivy holder was a valuable asset in the antique game. There was a complicated polished wooden thing in front of the couch.

"Is that a table?" I asked him.

"Now it is a table. Used to be a cobbler's bench."

"It won't collapse under a little weight, will it?"

"Oh no, no, no."

"All right, Martha," I said, "take the wad out and let's get on with the economics."

Martha tossed the thick package of hundred-dollar bills down on the cobbler's bench.

"Sit down, sit down." Carlos's dark eyes glistened as he waved us into chairs. "And what can I fix you to drink?"

"Nothing," Martha said curtly. "This is a business call."

"Oh, very well." He hunched his shoulders. "Very well." He settled himself comfortably in front of the money. "I shall begin with the background you know. In my business, naturally, one travels a lot on the trail of one thing or another, candelabra, pictures, vases. Before the war I spent much time on the Continent. I had many friends in all countries. Now a few months ago a friend of mine came here from Italy—a refugee, a broken man. His wealth? Gone. His wife? Dead. His son? Killed for Mussolini in Ethiopia long ago. His politics? You and I have seen many

like him. It may be I am of the same type. We ride with
the waves, we turn with the wind, we are"—he raised his
eyebrows—"how do you call it? Noncommittal? My friend
was once a man of wealth, spoiled soft. I have noticed the
difference in this country. Here men of wealth are spoiled,
but hard. They do not drift. They have direction, sometimes good, sometimes bad. It is in the air here, the need
to go on and on. Maybe you Americans do not yet have the
skill, the taste to make a fine art of loafing."

Martha sighed impatiently.

"I am getting off the subject?" He smiled. "To go back
to my friend. He was not a member of the Fascisti, but
neither was he of the Resistance. To some Americans, if
a man was neither this nor that he was O.K., you know.
My friend was naturally anxious for the American Military Government to think he was O.K. When he met Mr.
Seabright through official business he made the most gracious gesture he could think of—invited Mr. Seabright to
visit him at Fucino. My friend had also met other Americans; especially was he delighted with the entertainment
people. In his enthusiasm he invited them all to come to
his home. Harvey Benson and a young lady named Gloria
Hart decided to accept this invitation at the same time as
Mr. Seabright. Too bad. One day one way or another, and
who knows what trouble could have been avoided," Carlos
said musingly. Then he clapped his knee and his voice got
brisk again. "Futile thought, you know?

"So when Benson and Mr. Seabright meet at the home
of my friend first there is reserve, then comes the drinking, then comes the heated argument, then comes bad
altercation. By this time my friend has suggested a sail
as diversion. On the boat Mr. Seabright punches Benson,
who falls overboard and drowns. I will let my friend give
you the details of the incident. You will have it right from
his own mouth whenever you say."

"Where is he? This friend?" I asked.

"Oh, very close, very close. Can be brought here in few hours. Now you must be wondering why my friend and Miss Hart said nothing about this bad deed but allowed it, the next day, to be called a suicide. For the young lady there is a simple explanation. She is the type that is loyal to money first above every other thing. Make money available and she is easily managed. As for my friend—as I have said, he was politically on the fence. With a word in the right ears Mr. Seabright could make him into a fascist and no one would dispute it. This would mean the removal from my friend of the benefits and friendship of the AMG. Rather than have such a very bad thing happen, my friend agreed to Mr. Seabright that he would say nothing of the occurrence. Maybe this is wrong of my friend, but he had plenty of his own worries. No time to be a moralist.

"Now here"—Carlos raised his hands in appreciation—"here is where Mr. Seabright got a brilliant idea—if only it had worked. My friend would never have said a word, but Mr. Seabright was not content with his promise. He wanted to make sure. So he denounced my friend to the Italian Underground. The Underground had been irritated before this at the lackadaisical attitude of my friend. Whoever was not with them, they said, was against them. They needed only a very small lie to set them off after my friend. What happened, how he escaped, I will let him tell you. At any rate, he got to this country. He is very bitter, you know. I am the only close acquaintance he has living in the States. He tells me the story, but what can he do? He has no money, no citizenship. He is just a poor wop émigré; he is afraid to do anything. I, on the other hand, am not so timid. I set up a branch of my business in the District of Columbia and I come down here to look things over and make a plan."

"You mentioned yesterday," I interrupted, "that you planned to blackmail Harvey Benson's murderer. Then you planned to blackmail Mr. Seabright?"

"Yes, yes, vaguely. But I dropped the idea after a couple of months."

"Why?" asked Martha.

"I met you, my dear lady, and I made the grave error of falling in love with you."

Martha's expression never changed. Her tone was quite impersonal. "And why was that such a grave error?"

"It distracted me from my purpose. It delayed me, and simultaneously with my finding out there was no chance of your returning my affection I found out that this young man had already become so involved in the matter that I was unable to return to my original plan. I therefore approached him with a proposition, you know. You remember, Mr. Pike"—he turned to me—"our first conversation on Martha's terrace one moonlit night?"

I nodded. "You said this is a small world, and you were right."

"I wondered that night how curious a young man you were," he went on. "For if you were curious enough to track down and possibly secure the same information as I had, my information would become worthless. I tried to keep a sharp eye on developments, Mr. Pike, and later when a queer automobile accident occurred I was afraid that your intense curiosity was becoming feared in other quarters. Finally you went to Cleveland—I presumed to see the widow?"

"How did you know where I went?"

"That Southern female at the switchboard. She had happened to overhear your conversation with the airport. A most obliging young lady—a bit too plump, unfortunately. To continue, I had no way of knowing what you might find out from Mrs. Benson. However, I felt she was your only chance, since Gloria Hart would most certainly be whisked out of the city."

"You kept abreast of things, didn't you?"

"I was depressed, Mr. Pike. Very depressed. I was paying for the error I had made in using up time and emotions on a lady who was lost to me. Then the other morning I read of the terrible accident in the Volga Room. My spirits rose. In spite of my mistakes I get another chance. So I came to you with a proposition. You refused me contemptuously, Mr. Pike—but, well"—he smiled sweetly—"here you are, aren't you?" His smooth white hand reached for the money on the table.

I snatched it away from him. "Just a minute," I said sharply. Carlos's mouth dropped open and he gave me an aggrieved look. I peeled off one thousand dollars and put it back on the table. I gave the rest to Martha and told her to keep it in her bag.

"What's the idea?" Carlos began.

"The rest of the money is yours, Mr. San Martin, as soon as you get your friend to come here to Washington and talk to us himself."

"Why, of course I intended to do that."

"Then you can't object to our keeping the money until you do—since your intentions are so good."

"You want my friend tomorrow?"

"Yes. By early afternoon at Mrs. Finchley's. He is to be prepared to answer all our questions and to do what we tell him. Then you'll get paid."

"Well, I will do my best. I cannot force him to do anything against his will, you know."

"If he objects you'd better make up your mind to force him, Mr. San Martin—or you'll see no more of the money."

"But—but," he stammered, "this is not fair, not according to our agreement that I give you this information in exchange for fifteen thousand dollars."

I shook my finger at him. "Your memory is playing tricks, Mr. San Martin. Our agreement was for one thousand dollars for this information, fourteen thousand dollars for producing your friend and convincing him to accommodate us. You remember that, don't you? *Don't you?*"

He lifted his hands and let them fall. "I'll do what I can, naturally."

"You are to have your friend at Martha's house by three o'clock Sunday at the latest. He is to be prepared to stay until nine-thirty, after our broadcast."

Martha stared at me. "But, darling, we're going to call it off, aren't we? We're not going on with the show after an—"

"Of course we're going on with the show," I told her jubilantly. "I've just thought of a new gimmick—"

Carlos reached for the thousand dollars and put it carefully away inside his coat pocket.

"Now I shall fix myself a drink," he announced sadly.

He went to the corner of the room and opened a round cupboard which turned into a completely equipped little bar. "Used to be an old pickle barrel," he explained to no one in particular. "Maybe now that business is finished you two would like a drink?"

"My God, yes," said Martha.

20

At three-thirty on Sunday afternoon Martha and I sat in her drawing room avoiding each other's eyes. Finally I dashed my newly lighted cigarette into an ash tray and ground out its flame.

"They'll be here soon," Martha said softly.

"They're not coming!" I slapped my open palm down on the arm of the chair and stood up. I walked over to the fireplace and stared up at the phony surrealist portrait above it. "Whose nightmare was that?" I asked.

"A very promising young man, he—"

"Where is he now?"

"He was studying in Rome before the war. I've lost track—"

"You lose track of all of us eventually, don't you? We're all promising young men at first—"

"Darling," she said.

"I'm sorry I won't be able to leave any trophies behind for you to point out to my successor."

"Where are you going?"

"What have I got to hang around here for? I was fired, wasn't I?"

"Darling," she said, "maybe the plane was late. Give Carlos a half-hour more and then we'll decide what to do."

"I know what to do. You go on with the show and Seabright and everything as usual. You'll forget this little fuss I kicked up soon enough. It'll have to be chalked up to my overworked imagination. I haven't any proof, have I? For all I know, you paid Carlos a thousand dollars for a fairy story. Forgive me for being such an expense to you. Can't your lawyer wangle it as a tax deduction—for necessary entertainment in connection with your business?"

"Why do you say these things?" she asked. "To punish me for loving you?"

I turned, and when I saw her face, saw the cost of that admission in her eyes and on her lovely mouth, I was speechless.

A bell sounded downstairs.

"They're here." Martha smiled at me. "What's the matter with you? Isn't that what you wanted?"

"A minute ago, yes."

We heard footsteps on the stairs, and Mr. San Martin walked in, followed by his friend.

The friend's name was, he told us, Ernesto Gonzaga. This Mr. Gonzaga was about the most elegant creature I had seen anywhere—beside him San Martin looked like a cheap fop. The Italian was of medium height, as thin and brittle as a reed, impeccably dressed in a dark suit and starched white shirt. His clipped jet-black hair grew to a peak on his forehead; he had great velvety brown eyes, an imperious flaring nose, and a pink, firmly chiseled mouth. His chin was his only bad feature, cleft and receding too suddenly down toward his neck—giving the conventional impression of weakness. At the moment he appeared wan and nervous. As his eyes darted from me to Martha and about the room they seemed to float in a thin haze of tears. He watched suspiciously as Martha closed the drawing-room doors.

"Why are you late?" I demanded curtly of San Martin.

He shrugged with weary exasperation. "Ernesto is not easy to convince."

"What did you have to convince him of?"

"That you were the two people who could help him, that if he told you his story the wrongs would be made right."

"Is that all you told him?"

"That's all."

"All right," said Martha, "shall we sit down and begin our talk?"

Mr. Gonzaga perched himself tensely on the edge of a chair.

"What is it you would like to know, please?" He spoke in a high excited voice with a marked accent.

"As Mr. San Martin has probably told you, we would like to hear what happened on your boat the night that Harvey Benson was drowned."

"It is a very bad story." He shook his head. "There is nothing one can do. They came to my villa. I invited them. I was delighted with the Americans who drove the Germans back, back, back. The Americans did miracles in my country. Anyway, these three—Mr. Seabright, Benson, and a young lady who sang in the show—came to my home. There was not much to eat, but we had wine, plenty of wine. After dinner I say, 'Let us go out on the lake for a sail.' Was a beautiful evening, you understand. I cannot tell when exactly I hear the argument begin on the boat. I think this Benson tried to keep Mr. Seabright away from the girl. The talk grew very loud. They shouted at each other. Benson say to Seabright, 'When I get back to America,' he say, 'I will publish that story all over the country. Every man in every city and village, even a man alone on a thousand-acre farm, will know about you and the challenge,' he say."

"Benson must have said Challengers," I told Martha.

She podded.

"I don't understand what he is going to tell, but it makes Mr. Seabright very angry. 'Someone must stop you, kick you out,' Benson shouted. 'I know everything,' he say, 'I tell everything. You wait till I get back.' Then Mr. Seabright make a fist—very big hand he got—he punch Benson hard. Benson falls overboard. I run to side with rope and life belt, but Mr. Seabright holds back my arm. 'Benson cannot swim,' screams the young lady. But Seabright does not let go of my arm. I hear Benson call, then he stops calling. It is dark; we do not see him or hear him. He is drowned."

I could not help taking a long breath of relief and turning triumphantly to Martha. She was frowning, and her eyes were agonized when they met mine. San Martin was nodding his head up and down in fast little jerks of vindication.

"Go on with the story, please, Mr. Gonzaga," I said. "What happened after that?"

"Mr. Seabright, he turned to the two of us. 'Mr. Benson was a very unhappy man,' he say. 'Mr. Benson drowned himself.'"

"Did the young lady protest?"

"She just look with big eyes at him."

"What did you say?"

"I say, 'Yes, he was an unhappy man, he drowned himself.'"

"Why did you do that?"

"I was frightened. I wanted no trouble. With the war and everything we had trouble enough. My son, my wife gone, most of my father's fortune gone, everything ruined and gone. I do not want any more trouble." His thin eggshell-like hand plucked at the knot of his black tie. "I did not know what would happen. Mr. Seabright explained it would be the most simple. Why should I mix up in a fight between the Americans? And the man Benson was dead, you understand. I could not restore his breath, no matter what."

"So then what happened?"

"The body was found next day. American major came up to ask questions and hold inquiries. We say Benson went for walk after supper, very unhappy, threw himself into lake from the shore. Everything settled, Mr. Seabright and young lady go back to Rome, I never see the two of them any more. But I hear from Mr. Seabright again."

"How do you mean?"

His brown eyes turned hard and fiery. He spoke through clenched teeth, obviously moved to rage by what he was about to tell us.

"I hear from Mr. Seabright through my gardener Anton. He is loyal to me. He comes next night sneaking like a thief, knocking on the window. 'What is it?' I ask him. He tells me the Underground are after me. I ask what for. 'For being a fascist,' he tells me, 'for helping the Germans.' 'But, Anton, you know I am not a fascist,' I say. 'But they cannot be reasoned with; they believe what the American told Dino.' 'What American?' 'The big one with the yellow hair who was here for dinner the other night.' Quick I take what money I have, what jewels of my wife are left, everything of value I can put in my pocket, and I ride on Anton's donkey away from there. Before I leave the country I hear my home was burned to the ground. Nothing left." He gazed silently into space for a moment. Then he raised his fist and uttered an oath in Italian. "He wanted them to kill me," he whispered. "I like to kill him." He turned to me. "Carlos, tell me you can help me bring justice to this rotten pig. How? Now you talk to me. Now you tell me how to do it."

I described to him the radio show and Seabright's part in it and how Seabright was about to get a senatorial appointment. "The show goes out over a network all over the United States," I said. "Tonight you will confront Seabright during the broadcast and tell this story you have just told us."

"Tell this story over the wireless! No, no, no!" He waved his hands in the air. "No, no, no, I cannot do it! It will be bad for me, dangerous. Then the police will know I saw the crime and kept quiet. I will go to prison."

"That's right, Mr. Gonzaga. You were an accessory after the fact—you saw a murder and kept quiet about it. That makes you almost as guilty as Seabright, don't you think? A prison term might be considered light under the circumstances."

Mr. Gonzaga turned on Carlos. "What is happening?" he cried out in a hysterical voice. "You have sold me out! You have betrayed me!"

Carlos addressed him scornfully. "How have I sold you out? I do not even get the money unless you do what they ask. It is still up to you."

"No, it isn't," I said. "Either way Mr. Gonzaga faces a problem. If he refuses to grant our request we can turn him in to the police. He has admitted being an accessory before the three of us. We will be the witnesses." I argued with the Italian. "You have nothing to lose by helping us try to get Seabright to admit his guilt. Then you will see the justice done that you talked so eagerly about before. Afterward we will do everything to help you."

"We'll do everything in our power to get amnesty for you," Martha said. "You've heard of that."

"Listen to me, Ernesto," Carlos cajoled, "We will divide the money—"

"No, no, no, I don't care for money." The cords in Mr. Gonzaga's slender neck stood out as he argued. "I care for my life, for my freedom. I have been through too much.

I don't want any more trouble." His voice quavered and broke. He bent his head and wept.

"Mr. Gonzaga," I said, "we have all been through a lot. Each man's life has its share of suffering. We understand what you mean when you say you don't want any more trouble—but this time it is necessary to accept trouble." I hesitated. What was I going to say—accept trouble to save his soul? It sounded like a sermon. I hated him for forcing me into this preacher's role. I felt like shaking him by his expertly padded shoulders until his teeth rattled. But I had to make him speak—without him we were lost. How much power, I thought, each man holds in his tongue. "Listen, Mr. Gonzaga," I went on menacingly, "you have been on the losing side so far; you were a fascist and—

He lifted his head. "No!"

"In these times there is no middle ground, no fence, no no-man's land. You were not an anti-fascist, therefore you were a fascist. Many of your countrymen and mine died so we could be sitting here in this room alive. Alive but not carefree, not avoiding trouble, not permitting their murderers to flourish with us. You will do exactly as we say; you will face Lloyd Seabright in front of the microphone tonight, Mr. Gonzaga."

He shook his head slowly from side to side. "I wish to think about it."

God, but I wanted to get my hands on him; I wanted to close my fingers tight around that fastidious white collar and press hard.

"There is no time to think about it. You agree now, immediately, or we call the police."

It was ridiculous, like an aggravated father threatening a small boy—but no one was smiling. Martha and San Martin never moved their intent eyes from the Italian's face. All at once I saw them blink and sit back in their chairs and, glancing quickly toward Mr. Gonzaga, I saw that he was nodding his head.

Martha directed San Martin to take Mr. Gonzaga upstairs into one of the bedrooms, where he must stay until we wanted him. She said that I would be up later to go over our plans with him, and in the meantime she'd have coffee and whatever else they wanted to eat sent up. San Martin said coffee would be sufficient, and the two of them left us.

"Well, well"—Martha lighted a cigarette—"that was quite a little pep talk."

"You know I mean those things I was telling him. I believe in them—but when it comes to the words—I—it's foolish of me, but I feel unreal, like the hero in a propaganda play."

"Darling, I know. I'm the same way. I get uncomfortable, too, when I admit my finer sentiments. Do you know it's much harder work to say to someone 'I love you' than it is to say 'I hate you?'"

"You like to tangle with the tough jobs, don't you?" I took her in my arms. "Because you do it so well." I removed the cigarette from between her lips. "You smoke too much." I kissed her.

A moment later she said, "What do you expect will happen? What do you think Lloyd will do when Mr. Gonzaga walks in?"

"I wish I knew. He might get violent."

"Lloyd? No. That's out of character, but—"

"Wait a minute. It's out of character as you know him—but not for my version of him. He was violent yesterday, wasn't he? And the time he ran his car into me and—"

"Darling, forgive me." She looked at me with stricken eyes. "You know with me he has always been so poised, so much master of the situation. I used to admire him for it, the cool way he handled everything, never dreaming how uncontrollably savage he was underneath. Alec, remember he can put on a cool and cagey act—you'd better be careful. He thinks fast on his feet. He's liable to shut up and spoil your plan, or he might even outtalk you."

"If this Ernesto Gonzaga follows my instructions, Lloyd will have a hard time outtalking the two of us," I told her. "No, I think from what he tried yesterday he's actually desperate. He's near the breaking point. And don't forget, we've got surprise on our side. Lloyd thinks Gonzaga is dead, bumped off by the Underground—then to see him alive before his eyes—that ought to shock him into giving himself away. Incidentally, that was a rather vile idea, wasn't it? Using the Resistance fighters to do his murdering for him?"

"Horrible. God, I can't connect it—I'm so confused."

We heard the faint ring of the doorbell downstairs. "That must be Hal Corbett," I said. "I'll go down and help him with his stuff. You send the governor a telegram right away."

"What shall I say?"

"Tell him he's got to listen in tonight, say something— Oh hell, you know how to be persuasive—just make sure he's at that radio." I started for the door.

"Darling," Martha called, "I'm scared."

I turned around. "So am I—but I feel wonderful. Say, did I ever tell you about the dream I had that night—after I met you in front of the National Theater? No? Remind me to tell it to you later."

I helped Hal lug his apparatus upstairs into the library. When he saw the book-laden shelves he popped his eyes with mock amazement.

"Mean to tell me she curls up at night with these?"

"She knows how to read," I told him.

"Minds too?" He turned a Groucho Marx leer onto the doorway. "Where is she?"

"Why don't you get yourself a comedy spot? You're corny enough."

"Listen, ole bean, don't forget I knew you when you were out on the streets."

"I'll be back out on them, too, if things don't pan out tonight."

"What's the dope, Alec?" His tone turned serious.

"I want two mikes set up—the usual one and one hidden, and I mean hidden."

"What's it all about?"

"Hal, that's why I asked especially to have you do the setting up tonight. I figured you knew me well enough to give me a chance without asking questions. Everything will be explained on the show, and if it isn't I'll give you my personal interpretation later. Would you just do it for me and take my word for it that that's the way it's got to be?"

"If you say so, Alec. Anything the matter?"

"Plenty. Now where'll we put the second one? Behind the books is out. It's got to get perfect reception."

He walked around the room, tapping his lower lip with his forefinger in his customary attitude of deep thought. Finally he stopped in front of a floor lamp with a big parchment shade.

"How about this? We can move it anywhere we want."

"Won't the wire show along the base there?"

"Not when I get through. You know, I've fixed up something like this before."

"Have you?"

"Yeah, a guy who lived across the hall from me got suspicious of his wife once. He was some kind of government tax clerk and he was out on the road five days a week, and what did he have to do at night but sit around worrying about his wife. So he got the idea of planting a mike in the living room, see, and then pretending he was leaving town, but instead he came over to my room to listen in to the other end to hear what kind of entertaining she did while he was away. So there was a floor lamp near the davenport, see, and I put the mike in it. A neat job, let me tell you."

"What happened? Did he hear anything?"

"Naw. You know why? Because the only guy she ever entertained was me."

He got to work with his cords and plugs. "I sure was sorry," he said, shaking his head, "when the Republicans got swept out of here and they moved back to Salt Lake City."

I assured him that I wasn't having him hide this mike for any similar reason. I told him to be positive that when we went on the air he'd be prepared to open this one if anything went wrong with the one we were using. He raised his eyebrows at that, but he didn't ask any more questions. That was one thing about Hal—even if some women's husbands couldn't, I could trust him.

21

The party looked to me that night like one of those underwater ballet extravaganzas Hollywood cooks up sometimes. In the green-walled rooms the guests were going through motions as formal as figures in a dance: the turning of heads as each newcomer mounted the crest of the stairway, the groups forming and re-forming the arms lifted for greeting, for slaps on the back, for the secret caress, the continuous juggling of highball glass and cigarettes, the toothy, mirthless grimaces.

Lloyd Seabright, his spanked-looking pink skin fresh and shining, his eyes and smile full of the spurious warmth I had come to detest, seemed carefree as ever. This night I did not intend to avoid him; this night I had reason at last to be relaxed in his presence, for now it was I and not he who was calling the shots and planning the next move. When he and his wife were at the buffet I maneuvered myself through the crowd around them. Lloyd gave me a hearty welcome, and his blue eyes lighted with what seemed like such genuine welcome that for a fraction of a second my confidence wavered. He was such a good actor; as Martha had said, "so much master of the situation."

Alice Seabright waved her glass in my face and grinned.

"I hear you had quite a little tumble yesterday, Mr. Pike."

"You can't ride those stable nags," Lloyd said. "They're half crazy from being hired out to anyone who comes along."

"I've had pretty good luck with them until yesterday," I replied evenly.

Alice Seabright peeped at me over the rim of her glass. "How are you feeling, Mr. Pike?"

"A bit stiff. I seem constantly to be feeling a bit stiff these days." I gave her what I hoped was a frank boyish smile. "You know," I went on, "the queer thing is that all through the war I felt so vulnerable; I thought every bullet and shell was heading straight for me. But since I've been home none of these accidents touch me; I'm beginning to feel indestructible."

Mrs. Seabright gave me a long slow stare, starting at my feet and moving upward, and for an instant my skin prickled under it. There was an ominous shine to the pupils of her eyes. Maybe I shouldn't be boasting just yet, I thought. Mrs. Seabright drained her glass and snatched a fresh one from the tray of a passing waiter. It's alcohol that makes her look like that, I told myself; she's as tight as usual.

"By the way," I said to Lloyd, "a miracle happened and I got my car back today. You can send for the station wagon any time." I took the keys out of my pocket and offered them to him.

Alice Seabright said, "I'll take care of them." She opened a small brocaded evening pouch suspended from a cord around her wrist, and the keys made a small metallic ring against something as she tucked them inside.

"You'll see that I get a bill, of course," Lloyd said.

"Oh yes. We'll have a complete accounting," I told him.

At last it was time to get ready for the broadcast. Martha and I rounded up our guests, the Cabinet member, the oriental Ambassador, the girl journalist, the congressman,

and with Enid Hoyt and Lloyd Seabright took them into
the library. Except for the floor lamp with the parchment
shade standing directly behind my place, the setup was the
same as usual: several chairs around a table, in the center
of which was the microphone. From behind his transmitter in the corner Hal winked at me. I instructed everybody
about the seating arrangements, putting Lloyd opposite
me and next to a vacant chair. Enid hopped up and came
over toward the lamp.

"Here, why don't you light this?" she asked. "You'll see
better—"

"No, no." I jerked my arm out and blocked her way.
"Don't bother with it," I said emphatically. "I'm not going
to use these notes anyway."

I took the two or three typed pages of script which
Martha and I had worked over several days before, crumpled them, and tossed them into a wastebasket. Lloyd's
eyes followed my movements, but his face betrayed no surprise. All right, I thought, we'll soon see how permanent
a mask that is. The announcer, a narrow-chested little
fellow with an incongruously vibrant, chesty voice, came
over and moved the mike to the edge of the table. He held
his watch in his hand, and when Hal gave him the signal
he began to speak. "It's Sunday night on S Street!" he announced in that tone of excited expectancy that had made
him famous—and we were on the air.

We went through the preliminaries as usual, giving our
listeners an over-all picture of the affair, of the people
present, of the food served, the gowns worn. There was
the usual spontaneous banter back and forth between our
guests. The show started off exactly as it had the preceding
two times.

When Martha and I had planned the discarded script
the first serious topic for discussion was the looming strike
situation. It had been slanted toward our guest member of

the President's Cabinet, who had once been a prominent labor lawyer. I ignored that topic and all the others we had decided upon between us and plunged into a question about the Paris proposal to change the frontier between Italy and France. The girl journalist immediately came up with a firm argument against the change, quoting an interview she had recently had with Sumner Welles. The congressman announced that he felt that Italy should be allowed to retain the South Tyrol and Trieste, too, and that its border with Jugoslavia should be the Wilson Line.

This led us into a discussion of the Wilson proposals after the last war, and though I attempted several times to draw Lloyd into the conversation he passed on the questions I handed him as if they were literal hot potatoes. He wasn't sure, he said, what was contained in Wilson's famous appeal to the Italian people in 1919; no, he said, he didn't recall exactly what demands Orlando made for Italy at the Paris Conference of that year; well, he said, he felt unable to put his finger exactly on the Jugoslavian counterclaims after the last war or even now. It was apparent that on a subject for which he had not prepared Lloyd Seabright was no better informed than the average man; his memory was, if anything, a little worse.

The others filled in for him, and after a short discussion I said, "At any rate, Italy today is again an extremely sore spot in Europe, and I'm glad to announce that we have an unexpected guest here tonight." In spite of myself my voice trembled. I saw Lloyd's eyes narrow and scan my face and Martha's anxious glance. I cleared my throat. "A gentleman is here tonight," I said, "who has recently arrived from Italy. I think he can give us a firsthand account of how the Italians feel about these things as of now."

These words were our signal, and just as I finished them the door opened and in walked Mr. Gonzaga. I had a fine thrill of triumph as the color drained out of Lloyd's face and the Italian, himself deathly pale, walked toward us.

"I want to introduce Mr. Ernesto Gonzaga," I said into the mike. The Italian bowed to the people in the room and took the chair I pointed out next to Lloyd. The fingertips and knuckles on Lloyd's big hands whitened as he gripped the table. He turned his head slowly for a horror-stricken close-up of Gonzaga's profile. I thought, I am looking at a man who is looking at a ghost.

Mr. Gonzaga began to speak. "Mr. Pike," he said in his high tense voice, "I see you have here an authority on my country, a man who has visited me at my home in Italy, Mr. Lloyd Seabright."

"Oh no, Ernesto." Lloyd tried to smile, but his face retained its pallor. "My short trip during the war hardly makes me an authority. Tell me, Ernesto—tell me," he stammered, "how—how do you like the United States?" He grasped at the change of subject like the drowning man at the proverbial straw."

"I like it," Mr. Gonzaga told him. "It is pleasant to see so many well-fed people."

"Haven't the supplies brought in by UNRRA improved the food situation in your country?" asked the journalist.

"No, not yet." Mr. Gonzaga turned his sad brown eyes on her. "Many people still die of starvation. One gets used to seeing them drop on the streets. War makes one accustomed to most kinds of death, except"—his eyes traveled to Lloyd's face—"except murder. I must tell you all about one American casualty I saw that had nothing to do with the fighting. His name was Harvey Benson, and he was mur—"

At the mention of the name Lloyd had leaped to his feet. Now he uttered a strangled cry, picked up the mike, and dashed it to the floor. "What the hell is going on here?" he shouted at me. "What do you think you're doing?"

"Why are you so upset, Lloyd?" I asked. "Did you think Mr. Gonzaga was going to accuse you of—"

"Why, you—" He slammed his palm down so hard on the table I could feel the wood vibrate. "You don't know what you're talking about."

"I know what I'm talking about, Mr. Seabright," Gonzaga said, and his thin body seemed more breakable than ever as he stood beside Lloyd's huge bulk.

"You thought you had me out of the way, didn't you? Well, it is not that easy, Mr. Seabright. Here I am alive and ready to tell the world what happened on my boat the night you—"

"Damn you, shut up!" Lloyd's fist drew back and Martha cried out, but there was no need to warn the Italian. With a movement quick as a snake's he plunged his hand inside his jacket and pulled out a revolver.

Instantly there was a loud report from across the room, and Mr. Gonzaga staggered as if he had been punched, although Lloyd's fist was still in the air. Then the Italian moaned and sprawled full length at my feet. I bent to help him.

"Stay where you are, Mr. Pike!" Alice Seabright stood in in the room. She had drawn the heavy door shut behind her, and now she turned the lock.

"Alice!" Martha screamed. "Alice, put down that—"

"Shut up." Mrs. Seabright drew back her lips in that strained crazy smile, and suddenly I remembered the sound the station-wagon keys had made when she put them into her bag, the sound of metal on metal.

"That's a good girl, Alice," Lloyd said gently. "You saved my life."

"Put your hands up, all of you," she demanded, teetering a little on her feet and the gun barrel shaking in her shaking fingers.

I could hear a commotion outside the door and then a sharp rapping.

"Come on, Lloyd," Mrs. Seabright ordered, "let's get out of here."

"What do you mean, Alice?" he asked softly, and the old smile was back on his face and his skin was regaining its color. He kicked the mike aside and bent over Mr. Gonzaga. "Dead," he announced, straightening up. "You see, my dear, there is no reason to leave now. There is no more danger."

The rapping from the other side of the door continued, insistent and louder.

"What do you mean, no more danger? I am in danger!" Mrs. Seabright whispered from between clenched teeth. "I've killed a man. I've killed a—"

"You were defending my life. There's nothing to worry about. Just calm down, my dear, and when the police come all these people here will be witnesses that you shot him to protect me."

I looked around at the white set faces of the others; eyes wide, breathing in short alarmed gasps, they stood like statues, hands in the air. Hal's gaze met mine, and I tried to signal him to rush Mrs. Seabright with me, but he didn't understand. He rolled his eyes around and back toward the lamp with the parchment shade, as if to reassure me that the hidden microphone was open.

"I've killed him and you're going to hand me over to the police," Mrs. Seabright was saying. "Come out of here, I tell you, come out and help me get away."

"Please control yourself, Alice. You did the right thing. Nothing will happen to you."

"You don't care what happens to me. You don't care what happens to anyone but yourself. I killed a man and you want to keep me here like a cornered rat until the

police come. Well, you're not going to get away with it."
Her eyes bulged in a wild stare. She clutched the gun with
both hands to keep it from shaking. "If you allow the police to lay a finger on me. I'll tell them how you murdered
Harvey Benson—"

"Alice! You're drunk. You're insane!" Lloyd took a step
toward her.

"Stay where you are!" The gun barrel described a little
jiggling circle in the air. "I'll tell them you hired George
Harbin to kill—"

"Alice," Lloyd said softly, and then I saw him walking
toward her, one hand extended as if he was going to relieve
her of a glass or an ash tray and tell her to say good night,
it was time to go. But she wasn't holding a glass or an ash
tray, and her good night when she said it was addressed
only to him—was the bullet that found his heart.

Hours later, after even the reporters had left, I sat at
the white-topped table in Martha's kitchen while she filled
two cups with the coffee she had just made. I drank a
mouthful, choked horribly, and put the cup down on its
saucer with a fearful clatter.

"What's the matter?" she asked anxiously. "Doesn't it
taste good? This is the first chance I've had to make coffee
for years and years—"

"I know," I said, "you've been busy."

She put her elbows on the table and propped her chin
in her hands. Her black beaded dress was mussed and her
eyelids heavy, like a weary child's.

"I don't want to go to bed tonight," she said. "I'm afraid
I'll have bad dreams."

"By the way, I was going to tell you about an old dream
of mine, remember?" I took a hesitant sip from my cup.

"Darling," she said, "it can't taste as bad as you look."

"This dream of mine was that I parachuted down to the base of the Washington Monument and there was a man pushing a microphone into my face and saying to me, 'I'm taking an important poll, sir. The question is: Why do you go on living?'"

"What did you say?"

"Nothing. I woke up scared. The question really stumped me. This afternoon when I told you I felt wonderful it was because suddenly, through this Benson affair, I've found the answer. It's hard to explain. It's conscience or the voice inside or whatever one wants to call it. The good feeling of being responsible to oneself. I didn't know why I kept on breathing. Now every breath is worthwhile."

"Don't look so embarrassed, darling," she said gently. "I understand what you mean."

"And while we're discussing questions and answers—I heard you telling Lloyd where I lived the night of the auto accident. How did you know I lived at the Webster?"

"I'd known for months. The first time I heard you on the air I called the station and they gave me your address and phone number. I—I couldn't quite bring myself to call you up, but I drove past plenty of times, hoping we'd run into each other."

"You did? That doesn't sound a bit in character."

"That's what's nice about my character. It's so flexible."

"One more thing I want to ask you. Why didn't you show up for our date in Nancy that week end?"

She hesitated, and her eyes stared dreamily past me at a row of copper utensils hanging above the stove. "Those are very good-looking pots and pans," she said thoughtfully. "I forgot I owned them. I forgot what a nice room this is."

"I'm waiting."

"Because I was afraid."

"Afraid of what?"

"I had a premonition about you. Something warned me that it might end up like this—in love and in the kitchen."

"Are they both so unpleasant?"

"Not at all." Her smile was very broad and delighted as she picked up the percolator. "I'm going to get the cookbook and do this right."

I sat there on the tall chromium stool and watched her rummage in a drawer for the book and find the recipe. I thought that of all the sights I'd seen in my life there had never been one more satisfying than the sight of a beautiful woman with a flexible character making good coffee.

The phone woke me the next morning at nine o'clock sharp. It was Ralph Logan.

"Wow!" he shouted. "Quite a show you produced last night!"

I yawned audibly.

"I see in the papers that That One told the reporters she's not intending to go on with her little venture. Well, my boy, I'm giving you the chance of a lifetime. I'm going to let you have your old job back."

I yawned even louder.

"If it's money you're worrying about I can offer you twice as—"

"It's not the money."

"What then?"

"It's the voice inside. It keeps telling me that I really don't give a damn whether anyone buys tomorrow's diamond and ruby cocktail ring today or any day."

"What voice? Say, you got a hang-over?"

"I guess you might call it that," I admitted cheerfully as I placed the phone back on its cradle. A picture of Stevie's face, grave and reproachful, flashed through my mind. I'd have to do a lot of explaining about why we wouldn't be living together by this Christmas—but he was a fine boy, he'd understand. And maybe by Easter . . .

I dialed Lieutenant Kaplan at the Detective Bureau.

"Have you picked up the guy that knifed Winifred Benson yet?" I asked him.

"Not yet."

"I just found out last night that his name is George Harbin, if that will help you any."

"We must have been tuned in to the same radio program," he said. "But thanks a lot for calling, anyway."

Then I dialed Martha. As I lay back on my pillow waiting for her to answer I thought what an endearing instrument the telephone is—next to the radio, my most favorite invention.

Print-on-demand titles available at
CoachwhipBooks.com

Ebook titles available at
Coachwhip.com

Crime
is of the
Essence
Joe Csida

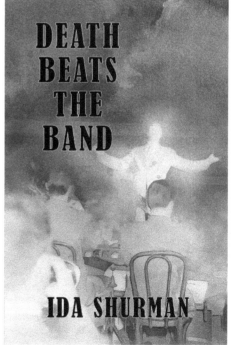

DEATH
BEATS
THE
BAND

IDA SHURMAN

MURDER AT DRAKE'S ANCHORAGE

E. LEE WADDELL

MAUDE PARKER

MURDER IN
JACKSON HOLE

DEAD
WEIGHT

ADDISON
SIMMONS

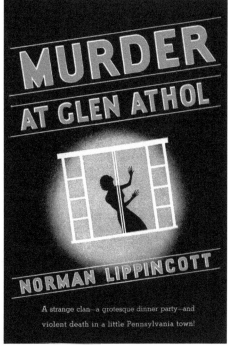

MURDER
AT GLEN ATHOL

NORMAN LIPPINCOTT

A strange clan—a grotesque dinner party—and
violent death in a little Pennsylvania town!

DRESSED
TO KILL

Emma Lou Jetta

MURDER
ON THE
FACE OF IT

Emma Lou Jetta

MURDER
IN STYLE

Emma Lou Fetta

THE MUMMY
CASE MYSTERY

DERMOT
MORRAH

MURDER ENDS THE SONG

ALFRED MEYERS

MURDER
A LA
MODE

ELEANORE
KELLY
SELLARS

CLASSIC RED BADGE PRIZE MYSTERY

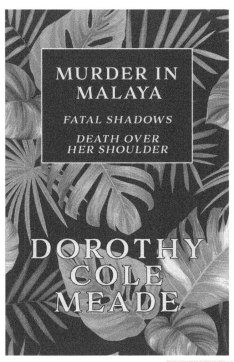

MURDER IN MALAYA

FATAL SHADOWS

DEATH OVER HER SHOULDER

DOROTHY COLE MEADE

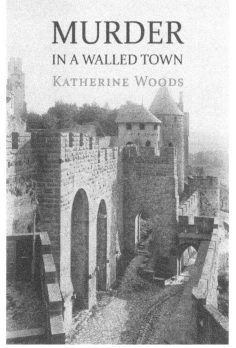

MURDER
IN A WALLED TOWN
KATHERINE WOODS

VIRGINIA RATH

DEATH AT
DAYTON'S FOLLY

MURDER ON
THE DAY OF
JUDGMENT

VIRGINIA RATH

VIRGINIA RATH

THE ANGER
OF THE BELLS

MURDER

with a theme song

VIRGINIA RATH

THE HEX MURDER

Alexander Williams

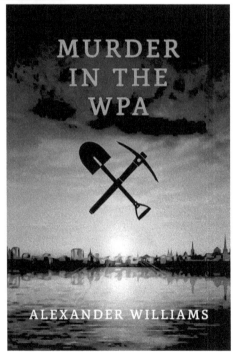

MURDER TAKES
THE VEIL

MURDER AT
ST. DENNIS

SISTER SIMON'S
MURDER CASE

THE MARGARET ANN HUBBARD
MYSTERY OMNIBUS

THE PHILOSOPHER'S
MURDER CASE

JACK R. CRAWFORD

Lightning Source UK Ltd.
Milton Keynes UK
UKHW042245050522
402577UK00004B/20